V&Q
BOOKS

Karosh Taha, born in 1987 in Zaxo, Iraq, has lived in Germany since 1997. Her essays have appeared in various literary magazines. *In the Belly of the Queen* is her second novel and won her the Alfred Döblin Prize. Karosh Taha lives in Cologne.

Grashina Gabelmann is editor-in-chief and a founding member of *Flaneur Magazine*, a site-specific, interdisciplinary and award-winning publication focusing on one street per issue. She writes psychogeographic prose and works as a translator.

In the Belly of the Queen

By Karosh Taha

Translated from German by Grashina Gabelmann

V&Q
BOOKS

NEU
START
KULTUR

Die Beauftragte der Bundesregierung
für Kultur und Medien

Deutscher
Übersetzerfonds

GOETHE
INSTITUT

The translator's work on this book was
supported by the German Translator Fund
as part of the NEUSTART KULTUR
programme, financed by the German Government Commissioner for Cultural and
Media Affairs.

The translation of this work was supported
by a grant from the Goethe-Institut.

V&Q Books, Berlin 2023
An imprint of Verlag Voland & Quist GmbH
Original German title: *Im Bauch der Königin*
© 2020 DuMont Buchverlag, Köln

Translation © Grashina Gabelmann
Editing: Katy Derbyshire
Copy editing: Angela Hirons
Cover photo: Shadèn Al-Alas
Cover design: pingundpong
Typesetting: Fred Uhde
Printing and binding: PBtisk, Příbram, Czech Republic

ISBN: 978-3-86391-364-9

www.vq-books.eu

IN THE BELLY OF THE QUEEN

Read this note after reading both parts

Translator's Note

The first time I read *In the Belly of the Queen* was when I knew I would be the book's translator. I started with Amal's story, for no particular reason. I read her story quickly; the absence of speech marks, the run-on sentences, the sharpness of her observations made me pick up the pace as a reader and I almost immediately began translating sentences in my head while reading, which hadn't been the plan. The unconventional flow Karosh has managed to establish for her character Amal is powerful and determined, which helped me get into the character's mind from the moment I picked up the book. Months later, when the amazing copy editor Angela Hirons began going through my translation, she remarked on Amal's voice: '…There's an "against the grain" feeling grammatically, which gave me palpitations at first…the palpitations passed once I got deeper in.'

I love that a character is able to give a reader heart palpitations and I'm strangely proud of Amal for being able to induce such a reaction. Amal's language didn't engender heart palpitations in me but I couldn't slow down – I translated her entire section before even reading Raffiq's. I wasn't sure whether doing so might limit my knowledge needed for translating but it felt right at that moment and, frankly, stepping away from Amal wasn't an option.

This isn't to say I recommend readers start this book by reading Amal's section; it just happened to be how I experienced the book. During the course of translating and going through several rounds of editing on my own and then with Angela and my publisher/editor Katy Derbyshire, I read the book from both sides several times until I was essentially reading in a circle –

sometimes clockwise and sometimes counter-clockwise and, by doing so, I was fully able to dive into the experiment Karosh underwent in choosing this unconventional book format. In her accompanying essay, which is meant to be read after reading both Amal's and Raffiq's sections, Karosh writes: 'On opening a book – with the clear allocation of the front and back cover – the decision has been made for us readers about what is the beginning and what is the end, and we accept that there must be a beginning and an end. A mutation of the classic book format can break open this unconscious, conditioned acceptance. *In the Belly of the Queen* is an attempt to challenge these automatisms; literature should break with traditions.'

I believe Karosh has managed to challenge with this book, not just through its format but also through the voices she has created for her two narrators, her use of grammar, stylistic devices and through the role of Shahira, Raffiq and Amal's object of fascination. Some descriptions of the book position Shahira as its protagonist but she isn't your typical protagonist – she isn't the narrator and we only get scattered bits of information about her. At some point during my translation process I became curious about the opinion of other readers and went on goodreads.com to read reviews of *In the Belly of the Queen*. Several readers were irritated that Shahira was announced as the protagonist of the book but then, in their opinion, only took on a small role. A few readers seemed disappointed and confused. I can understand the irritation if a reader was expecting Shahira to be the story's narrator or for the entire story to revolve around her, but the character and the role of the character is more complex and subtle than that. I think the beauty of Shahira is her ability to take on a different role for each reader and every time the book is read. To me she is more like the sky: the sky holds the weather, lets it happen and isn't hurt by it – it just *is*.

That's how I feel about my translation – it just *is*. I dove into the language of Karosh's characters and never came back up for air until I was done. I translated both sections in one go without rereading what I had written. I only began rereading my work once everything was done. Again, it was because Amal and Raffiq's flow is so unique that it drew me right in and I just stayed in that flow. Both are very bold characters and I downloaded this boldness as I was reading and translating. I hope the reader will be able to feel into it too.

Schöppingen, September 2022

No one wants to fight Younes. Something gets knocked out of your body when he hits you in the temple – suddenly you're merely a shadow, your body's numb, food tastes salty, you run to the bathroom and throw up, and your fear of Younes grows. You could spread out a map of the world on Younes' back and still have enough space for a second Asia. His shoulders block my view when I stand directly behind him. I sit down on the floor by the others; they sit in a row and don't look at Younes, they observe him. He doesn't know any of this but maybe he can sense it, and it makes him lonely. I volunteer, stand up, try to seem as tall as possible. My mouthguard tastes sour because I forgot to wash it. It's too large for my mouth. I feel at its mercy because it makes my lips protrude as if Younes' fist is already in my mouth. My jaw will start aching after a while.

Walid shouts: 'At least he'll shut the fuck up now.'

The others laugh, the Czech student-teacher suppresses a grin. He's been training our after-school club for several months now, and the guys like him because he used to be a bouncer and amateur boxer, but now he's a Muslim. At least that's what he claims.

He says: The tattoos on his arms are his witnesses.

He says: You shouldn't erase mistakes.

He says: They show you who you could've become.

The guys nod thoughtfully when the Czech student-teacher presents us with philosophy for twelve-year-olds. He annoys me with his pretentiousness but he's well-built, and when he stands up, he's scary. Younes doesn't think about the teacher; his gaze rests on me but not in an intense way – he's grateful because I saved him from standing in the ring on his own. We're fighting against each other, Younes, not together, I want to remind him. We're not in year five any more, when I'd punch anyone who insulted Younes in the stomach. I don't need to do that any more, because Younes has grown into a mountain.

Half of Younes' face disappears behind his guard. He's careful despite his bulk – he's been beaten up too many times in the past. The fear grew as his bones did, and that's why every move's carefully considered. When he strikes, he darts forward with nifty footwork: his whole body moves in unison. My punches ricochet off his gloves. If I want to hit Younes, I have to get past his guard.

'Make yourself smaller!' shouts the teacher.

'Don't let down your guard!' says the teacher.

Younes fought his whole life to keep up his guard, and somehow, he always failed because we all knew how to attack Younes. But of course, the Czech is talking about me now.

Attack surface – you don't need to know the term to know what it means; that's how exact the word is, like a perfectly trimmed hedge. Boxing's about risk, I want to shout back, but at that moment Younes' strikes my jaw, and I'm thankful he's wearing gloves.

The Czech thinks he has to give me advice after the first round: says I have too much anger in my belly, that I have to keep a clear mind, that it's about strategy, not street fighting.

'Real wise,' I say. He ignores me and turns to Younes to praise him. Younes is thrilled on the inside; I can see how much effort it's taking him to keep any hint of satisfaction from his face. No one should get the impression Younes craves praise from a grown man, that he wags his tail like a dog when someone bothers to pet his head. Younes has reached a point where he fights off praise and punches in equal measure. No one should think Younes has been neglected in any way, that Younes seeks approval. Younes stands like a monument. I want to turn around and tell the guys to take a photo of him for future generations.

I'm more careful in the second round, keep my distance, and

the mountain approaches me. I force myself not to run away – it would give the guys something to laugh about. They'd definitely take a photo of that for future generations. Now, as if my thoughts were laid out for Younes to read, he deliberately misses. His glove grazes my left ear, which burns from the friction. I know Younes never misses with his dominant hand, never. He stares into my eyes for two seconds, tells me he knows what I was thinking, knows my train of thoughts, would never hurt me; in those two seconds he tells me I'm his one true friend, says I can count on you, says a lot more in those two seconds, and gives me another two seconds without protecting himself – a mistake so I can hit him, so I'll be the victor who managed to hit Younes. I don't do him the favour of letting me win like a little kid so he can feel good. You don't beat someone who can carry two Asias on their back; at most, you touch them as lightly as you would the Kaaba. Even a successful strike's unlikely – the guys would think Younes had gone easy on me because we're friends. The only honourable way of leaving the ring is to be on the defensive. A boring fight, nothing for future generations to remember, just a Thursday afternoon. The teacher makes us shake hands after the fight, as if he's creating world peace. I offer Younes a high-five because handshakes are for people who only respect each other because they have to.

The teacher wants to analyse the fight, asks the guys if Younes and I made mistakes we can avoid next time. The guys stare at us with their fish eyes, open their mouths but only air escapes. Then Walid speaks: 'Raffiq needs to grow a bit more.'

The guys laugh, and again the teacher suppresses his fucking grin as if he doesn't want to offend me, not knowing that this actually offends me even more.

'You let down your guard a couple of times, Younes,' he says.

We're allowed to practise with a sparring partner. We spread out across the gym, but some of the Turkish guys gather around the Czech teacher, thrilled that a Christian has turned Muslim – as if that upgrades Islam. They listen to him as he recites the hadith to justify his views. Younes and I try not to let his conversion impress us, and we stay away from him. But today I want to give him a hard time, and that's why I approach the group and hear the teacher going on about women. Even the way he starts his sentence annoys me: 'Our prophet Muhammad –'

'Your prophet's Jesus, man!', I shout at him. The Turks look at me annoyed. Younes laughs, and the teacher continues: 'Our prophet Muhammad, ṣallā llāhu ʿalayhī wa-ʾālihī wa-sallama, said paradise lies beneath the feet of mothers, and that's why –'

'What if a mother's a whore?' Younes asks, and because the mountain hardy ever speaks, no one's annoyed with him. If someone else had asked the question, everyone would've jumped on him, buried him beneath laughter and shouts, but as I said, Younes is Younes – who would dare get annoyed? I enjoy the tension in the air and the stillness Younes has forced on everyone. The teacher's head is about to explode. But he's the first to react and says, 'Excuse me?' His eyes become less blue.

'What does the prophet say about how to treat a mother who's a whore?'

'It's pretty disrespectful to speak about mothers like that, Younes.'

'But if it's the truth.' Younes insists there are mothers who are whores. The other guys expect the teacher to answer.

'It's still disrespectful.'

'You've no idea, have you? Anyway, I want to know what the prophet said, not some bouncer.'

The teacher, who used to be a bouncer and a boxer, and who still is a boxer and now a Muslim, has a lot of patience with Younes. His chest swells as he gets ready to answer, and he starts telling a story about the past, about a guy on his death bed. The whole village gathered around the man, who was shivering and sweating; even the doctor didn't know what to do for his pain. Everyone was at a loss because the dying man was a devout Muslim – he hadn't lied or cheated or behaved indecently, so why was Allah making him suffer? His wife and children cried for him and prayed that he might finally find peace. Then the sheikh entered the room, and when he saw the dying man, he immediately knew why he was suffering. He ordered a couple of village boys to inform the dying man's mother, as only his mother could free him from his unbearable pain, by forgiving her son's sins. As she forgave him, he died peacefully in bed.

The bell sounds like a sign from God, confirming the truth of the story. Younes is the first to move, and we follow him into the changing room. Younes calmly packs his bag. The others have started talking about exams, but Younes is in another world, and his silence forces me to submerge with him.

We live on the same street. That's why we always walk home together; we always have done, and we always will. Younes hates the neighbourhood, because it makes him walk with his head bowed down, shoulders drooping. No matter how big and broad he trains himself to be, a fleeting glance or a telling grin knocks him right back to the ground. Younes smokes so he doesn't have to talk. I walk next to him and feel him share his burden with me. I want to tell him life's tough for everyone, but then I'd sound like the teacher, so I keep quiet. A Czech guy who wants to teach us about Islam, who gets his knowledge from a pile of used books he bought online for five euros. The teacher doesn't know Younes, he doesn't know Shahira, who is apparently responsible for Younes' ultimate peace. And because the same thoughts are on Younes' mind, he lights another cigarette – he doesn't care that his lungs will hurt the next time he trains. He takes another deep drag. We say goodbye at the entrance to the flats. I watch Younes walk away, gaze after this giant with the broken back, until he disappears into his home.

I feel a bit sorry for him again. I can't imagine Younes suffering because the consent to die lies in the hands of his mother, a whore. The teacher talks too much – he doesn't know Younes, he doesn't know what happened in the past, and that's why he doesn't know what's happening now, who Younes is, who his mother is. The teacher can only run his mouth and quote old books on what he or others should do. I need to go to Mr Schandt and tell him about the student-teacher, who doesn't know Younes or Younes' mother, and who talks about Islam as if it were a wonder cure for any infection.

***

The annoying thing about Jamal's wife isn't just that she's Jamal's wife, but that her facial expressions and gestures are like a whole other voice accompanying her speech. There's not much to admire in my mother, but I do respect the attention with which she listens to Jamal's wife. Jamal's son is sitting next to his mother. He can't be older than eight, but his sluggish eyelids radiate the wisdom of an old person. I swear on my life, this kid's not thinking a single thought right now. When I was his age, I was thinking about how I could escape boring situations, but this kid seems to crave them because he's above earthly delights. He really deserves a slap in the face. He sits there with such indifference, he might as well be somewhere else, and the way he drinks orange juice out of the glass – not slurping, he's too wise to make sounds while drinking, not like his mother. He's got his father's eyes, a man who carries indifference with him like a backpack. My mother asks Jamal's son if he wants to go to my sister Newroz's room. They're in the same class but that's the only thing they have in common.

I pay attention to Jamal's wife when she starts speaking about Younes' mother. She saw that dêhlik, that bitch, at the mini-mart, touching the cashier Ramsy's hand for longer than she had to. She passed him every coin individually, their giggles becoming louder with every coin, and when she passed him the last one, he grabbed that dêhlik's fingers, which she playfully pulled away. All the coins fell to the floor, and the other customers stopped just sneaking glances and stared openly and knew. Ramsy grinned and blushed as he picked up the coins, and that bitch left the shop with a swing of her fat arse. Each sentence brims with spite and exaggeration, as if the truth alone isn't enough to condemn Younes' mother. Jamal's wife doesn't use the name Shahira. I don't know how the name would sound coming out of her mouth or which facial expression it would provoke. The name would probably make her choke; that's why she avoids saying it.

Shahira spreads in my mouth like oil. When I think of her as Shahira, I have to pull myself together. I can only talk about her when I think of her as Younes' mother.

And I hate Younes' mother a little bit more, although I always think I couldn't hate the woman more. But I do. I have done since primary school, since I saw Younes for the first time and he hid behind his mother and would've loved to hold on to her skirt if the skirt hadn't been so short and tight. That's why Younes disappeared behind her legs, holding onto her thigh with one hand, hiding his face behind her melon arse. She shrieked: 'Younes, get off, you're going to rip my tights.' She dropped him off at the school's entrance, gave the teacher a short wave, and stalked away in her high heels. Younes watched her leave and stood silently at the entrance, where the others knocked into him on their way past. It annoyed me because he wouldn't move away from the entrance. Surely he realised he was in the way, or was he stupid? Every morning in class, Mrs Blinder had to tell him to please take a seat. Whenever there was a new seating arrangement, Younes always chose the seat closest to the exit.

Younes' mother turned up at our door the day I beat him up. My mother didn't ask her to come in, just asked what was going on.

'Your son beat up my Younes.'

'I don't believe that,' said mother. 'Raffiq, come here.'

It felt like I'd forgotten how to walk, that's how slowly I walked to the door. Younes' mother immediately started yelling when she saw me. Like a cobra, she stretched out her neck, bent down and yelled: 'Why did you beat up Younes?' She pulled his T-shirt over his back to reveal a purple bruise.

'What kind of behaviour's that? You're not an animal!' She waved her index finger in front of mother's face. 'If your son touches my Younes one more time, God have mercy on him.'

'Don't bite off more than you can chew, girl,' said my mother – though Younes' mother was anything but a girl.

'Your son learned this behaviour from you and your husband. Animal behaviour – like animals!' she went on.

Both women yelled until their throats were sore, and we just watched them. The neighbours opened their doors to look, quickly shut them again, and listened behind closed doors. When Younes' mother strutted off, there was no one else to yell at, so mother turned to me and slapped me with a cold hand.

'Shame on you!' she said, sent me to my room and threatened that father would beat me too. But he didn't hit me; he just came into my room, where I was already snivelling.

'Why did you hit that boy?'

Because he always stood by the door. Because he didn't answer any questions. Because he was always sad and never wanted to play ball. 'I don't know,' I told my father. He sat on the edge of my bed and told me about Younes' family, and I didn't get what that had to do with me. Father ended his story with the instruction to never touch the boy again. But that wasn't why I stopped beating him up.

In year four, Mrs Blinder organised a breakfast with the parents, just before the Christmas holidays. Some parents baked cookies, others brought bread rolls, cheese, jam. There was chocolate milk for the kids, and a lot of coffee for the Almans, and even chai for our parents. We sat together at our desks and ate with our parents.

At some point, a girl called out so loudly that everyone froze. 'Mrs Blinder, Younes is crying.'

And then all eyes turned to Younes, who was sitting with a German family, a bread roll untouched on his lap. Younes whimpered into his hands. Mrs Blinder knelt down and stroked his skinny back, saying everything would be alright. The other parents asked what was going on, why was the boy crying. My mother looked at father and said in Kurdish: 'What has this woman done to her family?'

And a Turkish mother whispered to a Polish mother: 'His mother didn't come.'

From then on, I let Younes be.

My parents came to every parent-teacher meeting at school. Sometimes my mother sent father ahead because she was thinking too much about what she wanted to say and how to say it in German, so she only half listened. My father then asked her what the teacher had said, and she replied that she'd forgotten, and would quickly stir the pot or fetch the hoover. Eventually my father realised she hadn't forgotten – she hadn't listened. But she's good at listening to Jamal's wife and waits for a break in the conversation so that she can go into the kitchen to stir her sauce. She clears my plate, just like that. Amal's suspicions would be confirmed; she says I'll never be independent, because someone's always tidying up after me... But Amal also believes human behaviour is an equation: the father's behaviour plus the mother's behaviour multiplied by society's expectations equals the child's characteristics. And because we've been something like boy-friend and girlfriend the last couple of months, she thinks she can explain the workings of the world to me, and I pretend not to be interested, even though she's a lot smarter than me, but she doesn't know that.

My mother stirs her sauce and licks the spoon before putting it in the sink. It grosses me out and I want to tell her to stop it. But I restrain myself, otherwise she'd go off on one about all the things she had to do for me when I was little: Oh, you don't think it was gross when I had to wipe shit off your butt in the middle of the night, or when you threw milk up on me? Mother looks at me, asks what's wrong, and gets on with the cooking at the same time. She thinks she can stir something up in me with that question, but she can't; she'd have to look at me a lot longer, give me at least as much attention as Jamal's wife. I get up and leave the flat.

***

I want Shahira to lick her spoon; I want to see her tongue in action. But she never does, and she's always pleased to see me.

'Come on in, Raffiq.' She saunters barefoot into the kitchen. She's wearing leggings like the girls in our year, with her shirt just covering her butt. Every curve's still visible. When she's not wearing heels, she's the same height as Amal, and I could easily put my arm around her. Her dark hair falls in waves over her breasts and shoulders. Sometimes she puts her hair up – then you can see her neck, which is browner than the rest of her body. I don't know what her belly looks like or the folds underneath her arse. Amal's are white because she goes to the tanning studio. Shahira sometimes tans in the afternoon sun, but not often – it gives you ugly wrinkles and spots, she says. She used to sit on her balcony wearing a summer dress and let the sun shine on her glistening legs for half an hour. She fanned air onto her neck with her hands, and when a gust of wind blew up her dress, she spread her legs slightly to air her pussy.

Even though Younes had sat next to me, he only saw his mother, and I saw Shahira. She smiled at us, and today she's also smiling, but today she knows I see her.

'How was school?' she asks, as she takes the wooden spoon and points behind her in the direction of Younes' room. 'He never tells me anything these days.'

'Our boxing coach told us today that mothers take the highest place in Islam.'

'Oh yeah?'

'Yeah, and mothers can ensure their children go to heaven.'

'Not God?'

'Well, mothers are the key at least.'

'And what do you believe, Raffiq?'

She pronounces my name correctly, not like at school: once the word 'rare' appeared in a text and someone asked what it meant. The teacher explained: 'Unusual. Few.' Something like that, and Walid said: 'Like "Rareffiq"?' And the class laughed uncontrollably. The teacher also smiled, the wanker, just because they don't know how to pronounce names.

Shahira rolls the R and swallows the Q, which spreads across her tongue and crackles in her throat.

'Raffiq, you dreamer, I asked you something,' she says.

'I don't know,' I say.

'It's not a question of knowing, it's a question of believing.'

'Believing's the same as wishing,' I say. I probably picked that up from somewhere, but it gets her thinking.

Younes comes out of the bathroom, his hair still wet. He doesn't comb it, and Shahira has a go at him, teases him as if being a mother is just a game, running her fingers through Younes' black hair with her red painted nails. And she's proud because he's a lot taller than her and taller than me and taller than every-one in the neighbourhood. He won't stop growing.

We help Shahira set the table and sit together to eat; although I've already eaten, I eat with Younes and Shahira too. She asks Younes what happened at school today, but he just shrugs his shoulders, nothing special. She looks at me, her glance com-municating 'I told you so.' I feel like answering her with a glance which says, 'So now you're interested in what happens at school?'

Younes is careful not to be seen with his mother in public. Shahira's a ghost, a spirit floating around Younes – and she's always with us without actually being there, as if we're trapped in her belly. Eventually Younes will outgrow her belly, and no one knows what will happen then. And that makes us all nervous.

Younes was fourteen and at the market the last time he was seen with his mother in public. She ambled from one stall to the next and Younes followed her, always staying one step be-hind his mother, who knew all the sellers by name. The Turk offered her food at half price, packed the fruit and vegetables in two bags to be on the safe side – God forbid something might tear, he said – and laughed as he ogled Shahira's cleavage and offered his assistant's help to carry her shopping home. Shahira declined, while sampling another grape, and pointed at her son. This service wasn't available for the other women.

'I'm a regular,' said Shahira and confirmed Younes' suspicion that these looks and offers weren't common. The confidence which Shahira radiated as she strolled around the market, set up just for her, fed the other women's anger. They greeted each other, but not Shahira, and even turned away when she ap-proached. The women were props for Shahira, there to make the market more lively.

The Kurdish stall holder gave her half a watermelon, even though Shahira graciously declined. But the Kurd insisted and wouldn't take no for an answer. They lugged the bags home, and the words and looks of those men and the disgust of the other women weighed on Younes' shoulders so much that he couldn't eat for days.

***

Some guys play soccer in the town square, a few older men sit on a bench talking while twiddling their prayer beads. I see Jamal exit the betting shop with a coke in his hand, as if he only went in there to buy a cold coke. He greets us both; he's always polite to Younes and thinks he can tell me to call him uncle, Xalu Jamal. He thinks he's my uncle just because he works with my father and my father gives him advice. He usually acts up, but now he's all sweet, like I've got a bulldog beside me, and he asks if we want a coke as well. He says the betting shop's the only place that sells coke in glass bottles, that's why he goes there – he's yakking on, says coke tastes much better out of a glass bottle than a can or plastic bottle. He insists on getting us two cokes; he's really sucking up. I'm almost tempted to reassure him, to assure him I won't tell on him to my father.

'Yeah, get us two cokes,' I say, and Jamal eyes me with his lazy gaze – I can see his little mind is contemplating whether he should punch me in the face, but he's got no choice but to get us the cokes.

I don't remember when the first betting shop opened in the neighbourhood; maybe the betting shop had always been there, but because it wasn't a part of our life, part of our conversations, it was a void in the neighbourhood. At some point, during dinner, there was talk of so-and-so gambling their money away, the wife of so-and-so having no money left for nappies. My mother cursed these men, and father forbade me to enter these shops, and only then did I start noticing them. Someone must've opened the betting shops in the middle of the night.

That's the only way I could explain their sudden appearance. Younes is allowed to enter them because he doesn't have a father forbidding him, but Younes has enough common sense not to go in. Walid sometimes goes inside and feels all grown-up and talks about how much money he's lost and how the machines are rigged, and he just won't shut the hell up because he knows I'm not allowed to go. I convinced Younes to go in once, to tell me what it's like inside, and he came back out and shrugged his shoulders. The men stand at the machines in a trance and play a kind of 'Bubble Shooter' – their legs must be filled with concrete or something; he couldn't explain their endurance otherwise.

We take the cokes, Younes even says thank you, and Jamal pats him on the back, says he should get in touch if he ever needs anything. Younes would rather drown than ask for help, but Jamal doesn't know this, and no one knows Younes the way I know him.

The coke actually does taste better from the glass bottle. We get a box of strawberries from the mini-mart, and while Younes is looking for perfect strawberries, I watch Ramsy and struggle to believe how Shahira would hook up with this bean pole. But I don't know what Shahira wants.

Be careful with the ladies, said my father with a grin as he finished telling a story from *One Thousand and One Nights*. He used to tell me stories from *Alf Layla wa-Layla*. Sometimes he'd read from the Arabic version and translate it for me. Sometimes he went completely silent.

'Go on with the story please.'

He always said: 'She's asking him to do dirty things to her.'

'What are dirty things?'

'When unmarried women and men are together and get close, that's dirty. Then they commit a sin,' he explained.

When I heard about the German translation of *One Thousand and One Nights* in year nine, I ordered it online. One of

the stories really stayed with me because there's so much killing
and fucking in it right from the start. It's about a king whose
queen cheats on him with slaves. The queen has orgies, gang
bangs, bukakkes, gives blowjobs. The concubines accompany
the queen, wandering around the garden in their silk dresses
and tearing them off. It turns out that half of them are men in
disguise, who the queen keeps at her disposal. She also has a
tall Black slave who climbs over the palace walls to reach her as
soon as she calls for him.

The king's brother comes to visit one time; the men want to
go hunting, but the brother feels sick and so the king goes alone
with his henchmen. When she thinks no one's watching, the
queen calls for her big Black slaves. They fuck in the palace gar-
dens until everyone comes. The brother can't believe his eyes
when he sees the crowd of people fucking – and in the middle,
the queen with her legs spread apart. She lets a slave mount her
next to a rose bush, just like a common hooker. The brother
tells the king everything when he returns from his hunt. The
king kills the queen and every other woman in the palace, and
all the slaves too, as I recall. It's nothing short of a blood bath.
A killing spree in the palace. The two brothers leave the palace
on horseback, intent on finding out if it's only the queen who's a
slut, or if all women are. They start with another brother, who's
also a king somewhere. It turns out his wife is also sleeping with
everyone in the palace. Another blood bath. They go on a road
trip, but by camel through the desert. They want to rest when
they get to the Dead Sea, but suddenly the water swirls around
them and an ifrit rises from the sea, as large as the ocean is deep.
The two kings hide from this wahsh in a tree. The giant chooses
to sit directly underneath the tree; he's carrying a glass box on
his head, and he reaches in and fishes out the most beautiful
creature the two brothers have ever seen. The ifrit falls asleep
with his head on the woman's lap, and she looks around, bored,

and sees the two men in the tree. She suggests a threesome to get revenge on the giant, who's holding her captive as a sex slave. The brothers are horrified and scared the giant will wake up. Besides, they're good Muslims – they don't just fuck random women – so they turn her down at first, but then she threatens to wake the giant. And so the two kings are forced to fuck the most beautiful woman in the world, and they hate every woman in the world so much that they want to kill every single one. The older brother says something like: 'Even this terrifying giant who lives in the depths of the ocean and has his lover locked up in a box gets cheated on.' So they head back and decide to marry, fuck and kill every woman on earth.

Ramsy gives Younes his change, and his hands are shaking, maybe because he's scared, or maybe Ramsy just has shaky hands. I look at him for a long time and grin, for no reason, just to make him feel insecure, and he scratches his neck and wishes us a good day and asks if we're going to the lake, but we don't answer. Younes doesn't answer because he's the silent type, and I don't answer because I want to annoy him.

'What's up with the people here?' I ask Younes.

'What do you mean?'

'One guy buys cokes from the betting shop, the other guy sells strawberries. What losers.'

'They can't all be as smart as you, Raffiq.'

'Shut the hell up.'

Younes could do with being told to shut up.

We head over to the guys standing outside the tea salon, the same spot their fathers hang out at. I know everyone here: their parents and sometimes even their grandparents, I know if they have a permanent or temporary residence permit, I know which city they came from and why they're in Germany, I know what they looked like in primary school and later on in secondary school, I know what their mothers call them, I know what their fathers call them, I know what they're called on the street because it's me who baptises them, I know what they're afraid of and what they love, I know what they want to do later on and what they'll end up doing. Some know I know, others suspect I do: Halit kisses Khalil the Crow's arse because he's in love with his sister, Majit thinks he's going to be a rapper, Maher thinks he'll be a football player, the MaMa brothers will work at their father's greengrocers. Kemal and Mammut have been selling weed for years because they believe in the future of weed. Walid's the only one in the group doing his A-levels with us, and still he acts the fool in the group. Tobi's the Alman.

We say hi to the guys, and everyone asks Younes if his shoulders have got even broader since they last saw him two days ago.

'We should call Younes "the machine",' Walid suggests, but everyone ignores him. I ask Majit if he's uploaded his rap video yet. He says no; his father doesn't want him to make music, he wants him to concentrate on school. We all know how stupid Majit is; he's not going to be an engineer or a lawyer.

'Then just wear a mask,' I say.

'Like Sido, or something?'

'Like a ski mask, then it won't look as try-hard as Sido,' I say.

'Ski mask. Skimaskskimaskskimask,' he repeats with his stupid grin and says: 'Works, man,' and half hugs me. Majit steals. If he doesn't like someone, he rips them off. It's important to him if he makes it big as a rapper that we, his former crew, tell journalists he's always had a criminal aura and his lyrics are just an expression of that. As I said, Majit's stupid.

'You've got to create hype online if you want to make it, Majit,' I say.

He just nods: 'You're right, man. Myspace and stuff, but I have no idea what to do.'

'Yo, I can help you if you want, just let me know.'

29

Sanye walks past us with her mother while we're talking about Majit's rap career. Sanye's mentally a grown woman already; she was already unbearably mature when she was eleven years old, taking care of her brother, picking him up from school, carrying his backpack, probably checking if he ate his packed lunch. Sanye's mother can't speak German, which is why Sanye accompanies her to all sorts of appointments, and she does so with the patience of a saint. She translates truthfully at parent-teacher evenings, even if it puts herself in a bad light. Sanye's been a ten from all the guys for years because she also has a perfect arse – not too big, not too small, tight but still soft – at least I think so, because Sanye doesn't let anyone touch her, which makes her even more of a badass. When she walks by, everyone has to be silent, nod at most.

'Amen, brothers,' I say and end the silence. The guys laugh.

'Good thing she doesn't have a brother,' Tobi says, because he always says what we're thinking. He's allowed to because he's German.

'She's her own brother,' I say.

'Yeah, maybe she's a she-male,' Walid says and gets a reaction from everyone, he's good at that; Khalil the Crow insults him because Khalil thinks gay people are gross. He threatens to beat Walid up if he dares to insult another pretty girl.

'Chill out man, are you in love with her or something?'

'It's got nothing to do with love, you're just a retard,' says Khalil. 'You can diss Jenny, but not the pretty girls.' Khalil's never met Jenny but we've told him about her. Jenny's been rated the ugliest girl since year seven: her figure hasn't changed, she just keeps getting taller, like a stack of bricks. When the guys want something to laugh about, they get me talking about Jenny.

Even Younes can't hold in a laugh, though he feels uncomfortable with this kind of talk, as if he knows his mother's also running through our minds. But she's not part of the competition

– she's from another dimension. We say bye to the guys; we can't be with them for too long, but we can't be without them either. The girls are already waiting for us in the park.

'You really enjoy that, don't you?' Younes asks, and for the first time I don't know what he means.

'Enjoy what?'

'The way they listen to you, laugh at your jokes, ask for your opinion.'

'Almost sounds like an accusation, man.'

'No, it's not an accusation. I just noticed it. You fit in well here.'

'I'm not sure if I should feel insulted now.'

'No, Raffiq, you know it wasn't an insult,' he says, with an all-knowing smile on his face. Sometimes he allows himself to say stuff like that just because he's Younes. Some people think Younes keeps quiet because he doesn't want to talk, but I know Younes keeps quiet because he wants to think. He dissects situations and people, and sometimes, if you're lucky, like I am now, he'll share what he's thinking.

***

No one really appreciates Jenny's loyalty or is even aware of it. She's as honest as she is unattractive. I don't know if her friends notice they always go to Jenny when they have a problem. Jenny always finds the right words, Jenny puts her friends' needs before her own, Jenny never has a hidden agenda and is only ever interested in being a good friend. Jenny has principles; no tits, but principles, and Jenny doesn't know I know this and appreciate it. Jenny hates me because I make sure she stays a good person; the more repulsed the boys are by her, the more effort she makes to be loved by the girls. I make Jenny vitally important for the girls, and Jenny doesn't know this, and she also doesn't know

I chose her to be Amal's best friend; I let her into our crew. Jenny's smoking and is mainly happy to see Younes. All the girls are happy to see him.

Younes is a melancholy son of a bitch; the more he suffers, the more the girls are into him. They think the only cure for his pain is their compassion and love. Younes only needs to be loved enough to let go of his suffering, and each girl thinks she's the chosen one, that Younes will heal in her arms. Younes doesn't take advantage of the situation at all, and that's why he's a pitiful rather than a melancholy son of a bitch. He doesn't flirt with the girls, and if he does, it's not on purpose. He's never had a girlfriend, even though he could have any girl he wants; he could probably even get with Sanye – if he wanted to. But Younes doesn't want to. He wants to be decent, not in a religious way, but in a Kurdish-moral way. He's afraid people will say the apple doesn't fall far from the tree. It took a long time before I understood that. He never explained it to me, I just put two and two together, used Amal's method. First I thought Younes was shy, but he's not shy – he's strict with himself. When the girls aren't looking, when Younes feels unwatched, that's when he dares to look at the girls' butts and imagine what it'd be like to have his fingers wander over their necks. In those moments I grab Amal and pull her towards me. Younes puts on his absent-minded gaze then, thinking what it'd be like if he were someone else. Then he'd just be a spaz like the rest of us.

Younes doesn't get how much power he gives his mother by doing that. Every move, every gaze, every characteristic is all thoroughly thought through, but always the exact opposite of his mother. He forbids himself to do things he would've done under other circumstances. I hate Shahira for this, for having so much power over Younes just by being herself, which, in turn, keeps Younes from being how he wants to be. Her marriage was the first victim of her behaviour. Younes the second. At some point I'll tell Younes that, but not any time soon. He'll think it's weird I think about him being the way he is because his mother is Shahira. If Younes came to me one day and said, by the way, Raffiq, you're like this and like that because your mother once did this and that – I'd probably think he was crazy. You don't do that kind of stuff unless the person's begging for it. Younes isn't the begging type.

The girls in the park all offer Younes cigarettes, even though they know he'll say no. Even Jenny tries; she's got nothing to lose. The girls gather around him. Usually this only happens to famous people or gay guys but not regular guys. Younes is adored because he never says a bad word about anyone, he never talks about the girls, he acts as if they're all his sisters. He could lead a cult, but he'd be miserable because he wouldn't take advantage of the situation. When they show him their plastic nails and ask him what he thinks, he just says they look nicer when they're natural, and at home they rip the plastic off their nails because of what Younes said. They've stopped dyeing their hair, sometimes they even wear baggy T-shirts to please Younes, and I could slap him because he's turning the girls into nuns. Only Amal seems to be armed against Younes' melancholia; maybe it's because she's concentrating on me, taking a drag from a cigarette, her fingernails long and painted red.

'Habibi, please don't paint your nails so red,' I say, thinking how it makes her look like a whore. She pinches my belly, as if she's heard my thought.

'First, it's Habibti, and secondly, I love red.'

I explain to her that porn stars are associated with red fingernails – and she surely wouldn't want to be associated with that, as a little women's activist.

Before she opens her mouth and starts bombarding me with arguments she's memorised, I press my lips to hers. Because everything about Amal is soft; her lips, her breasts, her belly – she feels like Shahira – if I could touch Shahira.

I used to be able to, when Younes was bullied by the other guys. Shahira would cradle Younes in her arms as he cried. Her soft flesh smothered his sobs. And his back trembled from all the tears he'd been holding in for weeks. I was spellbound as I watched her hands move like waves over Younes' back.

Shahira's hands were anointed, creamed, powdered, warmed. I also desperately wanted to be comforted by Shahira. I wanted to look sad, to leave her no choice but to treat me like a second son. I sat next to Younes, by Shahira's left breast, where I could hear her heart beating loudly and slowly. I smelled Shahira, her sweat, underneath her arms – she smelled like salt and bread.

I wanted nothing more than to lay my head on her chest all day, my nose in her armpit, my fingers pressed into her soft belly. Shahira's softness keeps Younes from leaving her, from living on his own.

Amal and I lie in the grass, I'm allowed to rest my head on her lap, and sometimes I smell between her legs and make her laugh, but the most beautiful thing about this moment is the moment itself: we're trapped as if on an island – no one can escape, no one wants to escape, and I'm the only one appreciating it.

'Raffiq, what're you going to do after graduation?' She's been asking for weeks, even though she knows the answer. I just don't answer, that's an answer too. Amal always says it's important to figure out what you want from life, to formulate expectations and match them with goals to avoid disappointment. What seventeen-year-old thinks like that? 'Have you spent too much time with Sanye?' I ask; something must've happened between Sanye and Amal in the past, I can't explain her underlying aversion any other way.

Amal suggested I draw up a chart with life goals and expectations. I laughed at her but drew the chart when I got home, and

I thought for a long time, but my chart remained empty because I just can't formulate expectations.

'What are you going to study at university?' my father's always asking. There are too many options, I think.

'Raffiq, you won't move far away, will you?' says my mother. I hadn't even thought of getting my own flat, I think.

'What will you do after school?' Shahira also asks. I should study, they say, that's why I'm doing A-levels.

'What plans do you have after graduating?' Mr Schandt keeps asking. And what if I don't have any plans? I think to myself.

'Raffiq,' Amal shouts as if I wasn't right next to her. 'Raffiq,' she repeats, this time quietly, thinking and running her fingers through my hair. I don't use gel any more so she can play with it. 'I'm going to America for a year to work as an au pair,' she says.

'Where exactly?' I ask, as if it matters.

'Chicago.'

'Cool,' I say, because I don't know anything about Chicago, and I feel numb for the rest of the afternoon. I'm so numb I can't prevent a fight between Walid and Jenny, and Jenny leaves the park in tears and all the girls run after her to console her, and we stay in the park and punish Walid by not looking at him. I'm so numb I don't even notice the bad vibes between my parents until one of them starts screaming. They're fighting about dinner; my father doesn't like the taste of her biryani, he says it has no flavour, asks if she's forgotten how to cook. She ran out of Iraqi spices, so she had to buy German ones instead.

'But they're imported,' I say, and they don't hear me.

'I slave away all day and then I'm supposed to eat this grub?'

'Astaghfirullah. How can you be so ungrateful?'

'I'm ungrateful?' That's the sentence that triggers father's monologue about how grateful we should be because he sacrificed his profession for us: he would've been a respected man in

Iraq as an architect; here he's a regular worker at a logistics company. My sister Newroz is confused, her eyes darting between father and mother.

'I've stuck it out here for twenty years,' he says.

'You've been telling me that for twenty years, I'm sick of it,' my mother answers.

'You're sick of it? Then pack your bags.' And every time, they want to pack their bags and return to Kurdistan – that's until they come to their senses again. Before it gets to that stage, I put my hand on Newroz's neck and we leave the dinner table. In my room, she asks me why they're fighting.

'Sometimes people fight, that's just how it is. Don't you ever fight with your friends?' I try to drown out my parents.

'I do,' she says. 'But we always have a reason.'

'And grown-ups fight without a reason because they're frustrated, because they're annoyed at themselves, and then they choose to take it out on each other.'

'I don't get it.'

'Me neither.'

'When will they stop?' she asks.

And before I shrug my shoulders again, I ask her if she knows where Chicago is.

'No.'

'It's a city in America. USA. North America, you know, and it's really far away.'

She doesn't care.

'Anyway, maybe I'll do a year abroad in Chicago after school.'

She frowns.

'Maybe. I don't know.' I look at the piece of paper with the empty chart, where I'm supposed to have formulated my goals. I don't know what I expect from life. Why do I have to have expectations?

I turn towards my computer and type.

Chicago is 6794 kilometres from here, and that's just beeline. The time difference is seven hours, but Amal probably knows all of this and doesn't care.

***

The next day I walk up to Mr Schandt in the school canteen as he's biting into a sausage. 'Our boxing coach told us why Islam forbids pork. It makes men dishonourable and turns women into sluts.'

'Excuse me?'

'Yeah, there's a worm in the meat, which makes people commit sins.'

'Rareffiq, that's nonsense, you're much too intelligent to believe that.'

'No, really, our boxing coach has the facts to prove it. He showed us a few Qur'an passages, comparing statements made by prophets, with quotes made by scientists, and it all lines up.'

'Do you do any boxing there as well, or does he just talk nonsense the whole time?' he asks and puts his sausage down for a moment.

'We box sometimes. But Abu Hamza also tells us a lot about the life of our prophet Muhammad, ṣallā llāhu ʿalayhī wa-ʾālihī wa-sallama.'

'Abu Hamza? I thought he was called Mr Dvorak.'

'We're allowed to call him Abu Hamza.'

'Hmm,' he says and bites thoughtfully into his sausage. If only everyone were as easy to read as Mr Schandt.

Because our school canteen doesn't have decent food, we go out for kebabs, and on our way there, Amal catches up with me and Younes and butts into our conversation, asking if I'm ignoring her.

37

'No,' I say, making plans for the evening with Younes.

'I knew you'd be pissed off about Chicago. I shouldn't have told you.'

'I'm not mad.'

She slows down and walks next to Jenny, who'll console her and might be able to convince her to stay. I need to talk to Jenny.

All the girls order chips because they think eating kebabs makes them look ugly. Walid once told a girl: 'You look like a pig when you eat a kebab.' The girls stopped eating kebabs after that, or at least they don't eat them in front of us. They poke the hard chips with tiny plastic forks and dip them into mayo and ketchup. Their loss for being too vain, for caring what others think. Eating kebabs isn't about table manners, it's just about the kebab. Most people eat kebabs the wrong way. You've got to hold the kebab still and get your whole mouth around it. You don't bring the kebab to your mouth; your mouth needs to go to the kebab. When all your teeth are visible, then your mouth's open wide enough to take a proper bite.

The girls, especially Amal, stare at our kebabs dripping with grease, while we wipe tzatziki and cocktail sauce from the corners of our mouths with napkins. And then Amal starts whispering with Jenny. They're good at that. Jenny grins and glances at us with a conspiratorial look on her face, while Amal keeps whispering into her ear. They're really good at that, keeping secrets, whispering slyly, exchanging all-knowing glances and smiling cheekily. What did she say now, is she talking about us, is she talking about me, or are they just whispering to seem interesting?

A man as old as my father enters the shop and looks us up and down. This pisses me off; he thinks he can just stare at us as if he's looking for a suspect. He's Kurdish, I can tell, but he's not from here – I'd know if he were.

'Younes?' he shouts, and Younes turns around with the kebab in his hand, and Younes looks at the guy and slows down his chewing, tries to remember this man.

'It's me – Azad.'

And we all stare at Younes, and we can't find any clues on his face to indicate whether Younes knows Azad.

'Your uncle,' he says in Kurdish: mam, not xal – the father's brother, the uncle on your father's side. The father Younes waited more than ten years for, and now the uncle's here and he's smiling as sweetly as his face allows it. Younes finishes the rest of his ayran in one gulp and goes to get up, and we all push back our chairs to make space for Younes, and the chairs' metal legs scratch the floor. Even though no one says a word, it's loud just because Younes is moving.

His uncle opens his arms and gives Younes no choice but to greet him with a hug. Younes stands there, and all of a sudden, he's the little boy again who wants to hide behind Shahira's arse. His uncle asks him if he's got a moment. Younes has waited for ten years, he wants to tell his uncle. Then he grabs his jacket and leaves with this guy who calls himself Azad, who claims to be his father's brother, who takes Younes with him. He forgets his school bag underneath the table.

We watch them get into an Audi and drive away.

'That guy's rich,' someone says, and that's all that gets said. We quietly eat our kebabs, we walk back quietly to school, without Younes, who leaves not a gap in the group but a void, and we all imagine what Younes is doing at this moment. Back in the classroom we're completely mute, and we listen to Mr Schandt announce that the boxing club will be on hold until further notice. The Turkish guys get upset and ask why, but Mr Schandt wants to get on with the lesson. The Turks boycott his class by staying quiet, and we're quiet because Younes isn't there, although his absence isn't noticeable, because Younes hardly participates in class. It's suspiciously quiet, and Mr Schandt wants to know right now – right now, he says – what's going on, what happened, why no one's speaking. But no one can explain it to him. I could but it would take up Mr Schandt's entire history lesson, and it wouldn't be relevant for our exam preparation; that's what Mr Schandt would say. Younes' story should be relevant for our exams because his story affects us all.

Sometimes I was there when Younes asked Shahira where his father lived, so he could visit him. It made Shahira angry. Only anger ravaged Shahira's face, and I hated it when Younes angered her. She told him she didn't know where his father lived, and he should stop asking her, because her answer wouldn't change, and she'd do everything she could to keep him out of her life.

'He didn't want you, he didn't want you!' Shahira repeated like a prayer, when a tear-choked Younes asked about his father so he might go to live with him, so he wouldn't have to put up with the neighbourhood gossip any longer. I want to get out of here, he screamed, and that was his prayer – and at some point, Shahira agreed, said he should pack his bags, they were moving.

And that's when Younes realised he couldn't leave the neighbourhood, because he had to wait for his father, because he had to know if his father would ever return and take him in. And that's how Younes decided to stay and remain as the neighbourhood's bastard.

'Do you understand his dilemma, Mr Schandt? Then please explain Younes' dilemma.' And Mr Schandt would have to take notes and maybe give a presentation, and I would talk about Younes' uncle in the second lesson.

Younes had a lot of uncles, I start, and they all slept with his mother.

Even as a child, I spent my afternoons at Younes'. His mother always welcomed visitors while Younes and I played

40

on the PlayStation Younes had received as a gift from one of his uncles. The doorbell would ring, and Shahira would scuttle to the door in excitement to greet a man bearing bags of fruit, vegetables, crisps and coke. Younes' mother would pour two glasses of coke, tear open a bag of crisps, and tell us not to bother them. They'd disappear into the bedroom.

'Who's the guy?'

'My uncle,' said Younes, without taking his eyes off the TV.

It made me think what a selfish shit my uncle was – he never brought us bags of snacks. Another, much younger guy appeared a few months later – another uncle, I thought – and he gave Younes a plastic ball. Younes' mother stroked the guy's arm and guided him into the bedroom, while she told us, 'Play with the ball, boys.' My mother never let me play ball indoors, and I was happy this man had come and that now Shahira was letting us play ball inside.

'Why are they always going into the bedroom?' I asked Younes.

'No idea.'

'Let's go and see,' I suggested.

'No, mum locks the door.'

At dinner I got carried away, telling my parents that Younes' uncle gave him a ball, and asking why Uncle Baran doesn't give me presents.

'His uncle?' asked father.

'Yeah, he visited Shahira today.'

'You were at their house?' my mother screamed.

'No.'

'Don't lie, Raffiq.' Mother's wide-open eyes mean trouble and left me no choice but to lie.

'I saw him outside the flat when we were playing.'

'You can play with Younes, but never go to his house. His mother is one of those morally depraved women,' she said, and

I remembered what father had told me about the women in *One Thousand and One Nights* who do dirty things with men, and suddenly everything made sense.

Everyone flees the classroom after the lesson ends, and I almost turn around to look at Younes, until I remember his uncle has taken him. I wouldn't have said anything particular to Younes, I would've just turned around quickly to see if he was still there, and he would've been, because he's usually there – he's never sick, he's always there – but I always turn around just to make sure. And Younes looks back at me, says nothing, just looks back at me – and we both know we're there. Now there's no one for me to walk home with, so I walk alone and think for myself, but I don't think about myself; I think about Shahira who's about to lose her son. And then I think about Amal who's emigrating to Chicago. Maybe she doesn't know, maybe she does, but she's going to get laid by Blacks and Latinos there, because Amal has this caramel skin and you can taste cocoa when you look into her eyes. I really have to talk to Jenny.

***

Shahira touches her neck, touches the skin lightly; she has the most beautiful neck, long and graceful with a hollow you want to drink water from. And she keeps absent-mindedly touching her neck as she speaks, and her fingers rub the skin; sometimes they wander behind her ear to her artery, and she feels her pulse to make sure she's still alive. And she reveals the vertical lines running down her neck when she laughs, her neck slightly sweaty, free of any shame. She might as well be showing her breasts – that's how commanding her laughter is and that's how much attention she calls to her neck, which you want to hold your nose against. Shahira doesn't know about Azad, or else she wouldn't be laughing so freely about some character on an Arabic TV

42

show. She translates the jokes, but I can hardly pay attention to her, and I'm not into Arabic humour anyway.

'Younes!' I call, and he comes out of the shower with wet hair. I don't get why this guy always has to shower after school, as if knowledge makes him dirty.

You need to stay here, Younes, I want to tell him, stay here to take care of your mother who shows everyone her neck.

We walk to the town square and get a cold coke and watch little boys from the neighbourhood kick a cheap plastic ball against a supermarket wall. Someone drew a goal on the wall with a marker; the goal was already there when I was a kid, when we used to kick Younes' ball against the wall. For some reason I'm in the mood to kick a ball into the drawn-on goal, I want to feel like I'm eleven again, back when Younes and I knew nothing. Jamal's son is among the kids; he still looks like a clone of his wanker father.

'Oi, Bilal, pass the ball.' The boy hesitates and thinks I won't give him the ball back once I've got it. When kids fail to put two and two together, I just want to slap them. 'Yeah, pass the ball, mate, don't just stare. Come on.'

'It's not my ball,' he says.

'Just pass it,' I shout.

'Nico, can he play?'

What the hell? Since when do the Nicos in this neighbourhood decide who gets to play? Younes says we should sit on a bench, but I really want to score a goal today, whether Nico wants me to or not. The ball slowly rolls towards me. I take a swing and kick it hard. The ball flies in a high arc – not like Beckham, but almost – and because it's just a cheap plastic ball it hits the goal.

'Is that Jamal's son?' Younes asks and puts a cigarette in his mouth.

'Yeah. The resemblance is gross, right? As if he married his sister.'

He looks at the kid without any hate or anger. Younes and I are different that way.

'What did your uncle want?' I ask.

'He said how much he misses me.'

We laugh.

'And was he annoyed you didn't recognise him?'

'I did recognise him; I just wasn't sure. I didn't want to embarrass myself. You know what I mean?' he asks, and I do. I've always been by your side, I want to remind him, always there, although I never suffered with you. Not really, anyway – he was the injured one; I just got some scrapes.

'My uncle was the one to catch her. He's got a slightly different mindset than my father,' he says – as if he knows his father.

'My father was at work, and my uncle was staying with us for a week. He saw different guys leaving our flat and realised people were running their mouths. I was completely unaware at the time; she always locked me in my room and told me to play. My uncle told my father what he'd seen, what he suspected, what people were telling each other.'

He's talking about all of this for the first time, and he seems so removed from it; it seems to hardly affect him, because what he's talking about has deteriorated into a run-of-the-mill story, where everyone already knows every twist and turn, and the characters just have basic feelings like anger, hate, and love as they do in fairy tales.

'I don't know how I would've reacted, but my father stayed calm – no shouting, no violence.' He smiles. 'He just looked at her and thought it was incredible how she could look him in the eye and tell him the most banal things, as if she were the most boring housewife in the world. At some point my father said we were going to Kurdistan to visit my grandparents. I remember. We went to Iraq during the Easter holidays. Mother visited her parents in Duhok for the weekend; my father packed our bags in

44

the early morning, taking all of her papers with us. Her health insurance card was the only thing he forgot. We got on a plane and went back to Germany. He said mother would join us. It wasn't until we were back in Germany that he told me she'd cheated on him, she'd slept with other men, she didn't love us – but I didn't believe him. I cried, I wanted my mother, and I called him a liar.'

'And then?'

'She was smuggled into Turkey by her cousin; it was the only way she could leave Iraq. They went to Ankara, to the German embassy. She told the people there that her husband had lured her to Iraq and kidnapped their young son. And who knew what other illegal things he'd get up to? The embassy helped her return to Germany. When she got back, she reported my father for kidnapping me and made sure he wasn't allowed to visit me. When I asked her about him, she kept telling me the story of how he tried to break up our family, how he'd left her in Iraq to rot. And sometimes she told the story when I looked sad, as if she knew I was thinking about my father.

'I remember,' I say and offer him another cigarette. 'Did you tell your mother about your uncle?'

'No and she's not allowed to find out, Raffiq.'

'But she has to – '

'No, Raffiq. Don't you dare tell her anything!'

'No, man, I won't.'

He clicks his tongue and looks over at the kids again. 'A fucking health insurance card.'

I call Jamal's son over, take two euros out of my wallet and tell him to get us a large bag of salted pumpkin seeds. When he refuses, I threaten to stab his plastic ball.

'You're a psycho, you know that?' says Younes and laughs.

'That kid pisses me off.'

'He's not even nine, Raffiq.'

45

'Even worse – he already manages to piss me off. And what did your uncle want from you?'

'I don't know. I can't work him out. He went on about how blood's thicker than water and how he couldn't bear knowing I'm here on my own with no one watching over me.'

What a wanker, I think, and hope Younes thinks the same.

'Where's your father?'

'He lives in Frankfurt. Has a family. Two kids. I have a half-brother and a half-sister.'

'Why didn't he come here himself?'

Younes thinks and finally says: 'Him, here? Can you really imagine that?'

Jamal's son runs towards us, gives me a small bag of pumpkin seeds and seventy cents. 'I told you to get us a big bag, you douche.' I give him the seventy cents as baksheesh.

We eat the seeds until we get thirsty and our tongues feel rough.

Younes only knows his father from memory. And in his memory, he's a quiet, calm guy, generous – not with money but with kindness. If he weren't such a generous man, he would've held a knife to his wife's throat and slaughtered her like a sheep. His father could only be generous, Younes used to think, because he let his mother live, and now he doesn't know what to think of his father, and I'm confused too.

'I'll probably move to Frankfurt,' he says.

'And your mother?'

'What about her?'

'She'll be alone then.' I shouldn't have said that.

He looks around the town square, sees a woman leaving the mini-mart, sees the kids playing football, sees two men smoking outside the tea salon, sees them speaking to each other – maybe about his mother.

'She should get out of here too,' he says and spits out pumpkin seed shells.

The neighbourhood is no longer the neighbourhood if Shahira leaves.

***

Something has shifted between my parents, maybe something also got between them; I didn't see when or how it happened. My little sister won't know either, but I still watch her, concentrate on how she's eating. There's always someone talking at the kitchen table; everyone's got a story to tell. Usually my mother begins, then my father tries to join in, and I'll tell a story too, and if nothing happened that day, I'll make up a story with a punchline, and everyone laughs, and then Newroz tells a story, but it can't really be classified as a story– there are subplots, there's no real order, everything's equally important. I'm always amazed at what she considers worth telling, and maybe she thinks the same about my stories. Today we listen to our cutlery scrape the plates, the crunch of the salad, the bubbles in the water – a concert of everyday sounds. The whole cacophany of noise makes you want to mute the objects and set them to some melodious music instead.

My father slams the salt shaker on the glass table and startles us, startles us out of our silence.

'Why does the salt shaker only have three holes?' he asks, and I don't get what he means, if it's meant to be a joke, like: 'Why does the spider only have six legs? Because two got ripped out.'

'How's the damn salt supposed to come out?' he asks. He's not talking about salt shakers in general, he's talking about the one in his hand, the one he slams down on the table with every word he speaks.

My mother suggests he should shake a little longer to get the amount of salt he wants.

'Am I here to shake or eat?' he asks, and we all know he doesn't want an answer, but mother answers anyway: 'The food's well salted – why do you even need to add more?' And their fight seems to consist of lots of questions; my father wonders whether it's too much to ask to salt his own damn food with the damn salt, and mother's answer makes him yell, which makes her yell – and I wish the concert of discordant sounds could play again.

I leave the flat, I want to tell Younes that Frankfurt is 252 kilometres away, but then I don't walk to Younes' house; I just keep walking, enjoying the darkness and the wind; I think about what could be bringing my father's mood down, if one of us has done something wrong or not done something. I just can't put my finger on it, I've been too focused on other things. Busy trying to come up with reasons why Amal shouldn't move to Chicago, busy thinking about how I could convince Jenny to change her friend's mind to stay here. I looked at the page with the empty chart again for a long time, thought for a long time what my goals in life are, what my expectations are. It can't be that hard. Maybe Amal asked the wrong questions, not me. But then I'd have to think up my own, and I don't even know the answers to simple questions others have asked.

***

Younes is smoking on a bench in the town square. I wanted to be on my own, wanted to have the wind and the darkness to myself. Now I have to share them with Younes.

'Did you do the homework?' I ask.

'I'll just say I forgot to do it. You?' He offers me a cigarette. I take the cigarette without lighting it, play around with it.

'These are our last couple of months,' I say.

'No they're not. Something else will start and then you'll count down again.' I don't do countdowns. Sometimes Younes thinks he knows me better than I know myself.

'Frankfurt's 252 kilometres away.'

He thinks about his reply for a long time. 'Takes a few days to walk there,' he says. His voice is as powerful as Younes is himself – Younes has suddenly understood he could be in control of the neighbourhood; he's understood everyone could be scared of him. Younes sounds fearless; someone told him death is a hoax, told him there's another life waiting for him after death, and then another one, and he can live as long as he wants to if he doesn't care about anything.

'So you're really going?'

'What choice do I have?' he asks.

'Study here, stay with your mother.'

Younes lights another cigarette, inhales so deeply that when he breathes out there's just a notion of smoke in the air.

'You called the men living here losers. What makes you think I'd stay here?'

'They aren't losers because they live here, they're losers because of who they are.' I don't sound very convincing.

He inhales deeply, closing his eyes – maybe he's remembering something or dreaming of something, maybe of the ocean, or of not being here, of being in Frankfurt or Berlin or Hamburg, Munich, but not here.

'My parents won't stop fighting – I don't know what's going on.'

'I was spared that,' he says with the same tone of total indifference.

'It's strange. I mean, they used to fight in the past, but it was always about something specific, and now their fights seem to be about something else, and I don't think they even know what they're fighting about.' I look at him pleadingly; I'm ridiculous, but I keep talking and I end up getting his attention.

'My father's just looking for fights. Today he got pissed off about our salt shaker not having enough holes. They argued over a fucking salt shaker, can you believe it?'

Younes grunts, looks half interested, half appalled; he's almost happy to hear my parents are fighting. And then he has the audacity to give me a fatherly pat on the back. There's no sincerity in his consoling. Stupid son of a bitch, getting me to light my cigarette and burn my lungs.

'Come with me to Frankfurt,' he says.

'And do what?'

'We'll live together. Then you'll be rid of your parents.'

'That's not how things work, mate.'

'How do things work?'

'First I have to... I don't know, I have to ... That's just not how things work, Younes, you can't just go somewhere and start a new life and ignore everything that's happened. We belong here, this is our home.'

He laughs. 'You're scared.'

'That's just not how it works.'

'Yeah, that's exactly how things work. I won't repeat myself; either you come with me, or you don't. You can wait around and see what a badass rapper Majit might become – if he wasn't scared of his father.'

'We could live together here.'

Younes shakes his head. 'Raffiq, you're missing something really basic.' He puts his cigarette butt out on the bench, completely flattening it to be sure not to start a fire, so no one will get hurt. Before I can defend myself against his accusation, he starts talking: 'Walid and I were at your house one time. Your mother had made this aubergine dish, and we ate the whole thing. She had to make more.'

I laugh. 'I remember, that was a good day.'

'Your mother asked Walid how his mother was doing.' Now he looks at me, his pupils large and black for swallowing worlds.

'Yeah, so?' I ask, because he wants me to come up with a conclusion, which I can't provide.

'Walid answered, and then she looked at me as if she was going to ask me as well, and then she remembered whose son I am.'

'Mate, I'm sure you just imagined that,' I say, and I immediately regret lying to him like a rookie.

'Raffiq, you know your mother. She's the upholder of moral standards in the neighbourhood. What do you think she thinks of my mother?'

I shake my head, tell him nothing of what she thinks of his mother. Younes gets up, gives me his hand. 'Frankfurt, yes or no?'

I can't give him an answer and so I stay quiet. For Younes, every stranger means the possibility of becoming someone he'd like to be at that moment. It means he can be Younes a hundred times over without once being the Younes I know. He leaves. I stay on the bench for a while, watching Younes descend into the darkness before the next streetlight makes him visible and then invisible again, a magic trick.

And like magic, it's the morning – the sun lights up the world and warms people, makes an effort, treats us well, and then we get up, we're in a bad mood anyway, we've got bad breath, we hurt each other, sleep and wake up, and the sun's gracious enough to shine again.

My mother gives me my packed lunch in the kitchen and says my father called; he forgot his mobile, I have to bring it to him. 'Can't he be without his mobile for a few hours?' I ask.

'Bring him his mobile, he's in a bad enough mood as is, don't give him another reason.'

'What's up with you two anyway?' I ask. In the morning when your mind's still fresh, you can get away with asking that kind of question.

'Why are you asking me? Your father's the one who's losing it.'

'Why?'

She just shrugs her shoulders, busies herself with making Newroz's lunch and ignores me.

Jamal stands outside the block of flats, smoking and looking around. I could give him the mobile, but then it'd look like he was doing me a favour. I pass him without greeting him, let him think I didn't recognise him from behind. I know he's watching me unlock my bike.

'Aren't you too old for that thing?' he asks.

'No,' I answer; just no, no other remark, no annoyance. And the simple answer seems to annoy him. 'I already had my first car at your age,' he says, thinking he can embarrass me. And when I'm your age, I'll be driving a Mercedes S-Class.

Shahira walks past us wearing her tightest dress, her perfume following her like a shadow. She puts one foot in front of the other; no one walks like Shahira. Shahira's heels clack on the pavement, soothing Jamal. We both look at her as she walks past, watching her butt cheeks bounce with every step.

Jamal wants nothing more than to run after her. She's a planet and we're two moons who'd go anywhere with her as she makes her rounds.

'Those thighs,' says Jamal. 'You don't need a heater in the winter when you lie next to her.'

I'm still watching her and thinking how right he is, getting ready to leave, but before I do I say: 'Hey Younes, what's up?' I see the relaxation drain from Jamal's body; he turns around in panic and finds no Younes there. He gets my prank, wants to slap me in the face but I'm too quick for him. You're not more intelligent, you're just older, I want to shout at him. I cycle off, pass Shahira, smell her scent beneath her perfume; by tonight she'll smell like popcorn. I get why men want to mask their natural odour, but I don't see why women do. I'll ask Shahira.

Maybe I'll visit her at the cinema. She was hired as a cleaner but now she's allowed to sell tickets and popcorn. Her boss must've promoted her out of pity; Shahira told her a bit about her life. I imagine the two women smoking together, striking up a conversation. Shahira, unlike Younes, is really good at starting conversations. I need to ask her how she does it. I need to ask her so many things. Her boss saw a good salesperson in Shahira and put her behind the counter. She wears her name badge proudly on her chest, and sometimes she deliberately forgets to take it off, looks all official at home. Younes reminds her about it, not because he's annoyed; it's to make sure they both know their place and they both enjoy the moment. Younes and I take advantage of her job, visit her to eat popcorn – the only downside is it's an arthouse cinema and the films are shit. Rarely there'll be a good film playing; you know it was good if you don't feel like talking after leaving the cinema, when you want to play the film over again in your mind. Younes and I look at each other, leave each other be – we'll talk, but later.

I hop on my bike at the start of lunch break; I tell everyone who asks that I've got something important to do. And some believe me. No one needs to know that my father can order me around like a butler. Even Sanye asks me, and because no one can lie to Sanye – just like no one can lie to God, you can only evade – I squirm and avoid giving a concrete answer, promising her I'll tell her everything later.

His boss, Mr Bauer, takes me to him, says my father's one of the best workers he has. I see father in a forklift, stacking pallets in the warehouse. He's stacking them in a decent German manner; I ask myself why his German isn't as decent, even though he's worked with German colleagues for over ten years. He could at least conjugate the damn verbs, that's the least effort he could make. Mr Bauer calls my father, waves his hand to beckon him over. I'm going to slap him if he does that one more time. 'Mr Khalid! Come! Son here.' I look at Mr Bauer, who's suddenly started talking like a retard.

Father comes towards us smiling, and pats my back: 'Raffiq, my big boy.'

'Son hardworking like Mr Khalid one day,' says his boss. Mate, son box your bollocks. He says my father can have a ten-minute break, he's generous. 'Nothing works round here without Mr Khalid,' he tells me, but at such a volume he can't be serious.

Father shows me around; he's in a good mood, the opposite of when he's at home, he's like he used to be, introduces me to his colleagues, most of them younger than him, tells them I'm doing my A-levels. Seeing my father like this makes me think of Ramsy and Jamal around our neighbourhood.

'Are you the oldest here?' I ask.

'Old workers get sacked. It's not a job for all eternity. I don't have any chance of getting promoted. Only those who did their vocational training here do,' he says.

My parents attended these weird integration courses and eventually got German citizenship. Father went to night school later to get a German degree in architecture. In Germany, father's past was erased, his past was as invalid as an expired passport, as if you could lose your abilities when crossing a bor-der. He tried and failed – whether it was because of discipline, motivation, or it was all too much for him, no one knows for sure. My mother told me father locked himself in his room for a week after he stopped going to school. Mother brought him food, but he wouldn't let her talk to him; his failure was too great to conceal with everyday words. He downright punished himself by staying in this situation. He needed to withdraw for an entire week to say goodbye to the idea of being an architect in Germany.

'Do you think that twit cares if I was an architect in Iraq?' he asks, looking over at Mr Bauer. I don't know how long it takes to detach from the past. We go to the canteen and father grabs an apple, Pink Lady, his favourite, rubs it clean on his body warmer, as if the apple came straight from the tree, and gives it to me. I take a bite; a big chunk comes off and fills my cheek. The juice runs down into the corners of my mouth.

'Someone I studied with opened a four-storey architecture firm in Duhok,' my father tells me. 'He's reconstructing the country. And what do I do? I stack fruit pallets one on top of the other like a child playing with Lego.'

'Do you want to go back to night school?' I ask him once I've finished chewing.

He shakes his head. 'Kurdistan's being developed, the entire infrastructure's being renewed, the government's giving out contracts worth millions –'

'You want to go back to Iraq?'

'We have to,' he says.

'And do we have to come? What are you thinking? I'm doing my A-levels right now.'

'You can study architecture there and work for me. Eventually you'll run our office.' He sits down, points to a seat with his outstretched hand, and we sit across from each other like two businessmen. I look at the apple until the bitten part turns brown.

'Babu, I can't.'

'You'll learn.'

'No, I'm talking about living in Kurdistan. I can't even speak Kurdish.'

'You'll learn.'

'It's embarrassing to learn your mother tongue at seventeen.'

'I was thirty when I went to school here. You don't have to feel shame about educating yourself, Raffiq. Imagine living in a country just born, where everything's possible, where you can build something lasting – you walk through the streets and stand outside buildings you designed, buildings which only existed as thoughts in your head, and then the thoughts turn into buildings people can live or work in, where they can admire your creation.'

'I can do that here too.'

He shakes his head, looks at the apple. 'Isn't it any good?' The apple's all brown, a good sign, says my chemistry teacher, but it looks rotten now. My father hasn't asked for his mobile yet; it's still in my backpack and it'll probably stay there. He forgot it on purpose. I say goodbye, tell him my lunch break's about to end. I throw the half-eaten apple in the rubbish on my way out.

I only know Iraq and father's Kurdistan from the TV, and even there it doesn't interest me. It's a concept without any substance, and my whole body resists the idea of living there. I don't cycle to school; I aimlessly ride around the city. Maybe I should never go back to school, not do my A-levels, boycott father's plans. He should've thought about his return sooner, before I was born; he can't just turn his life inside out and mess up ours because he's unhappy with his life's outcome. He should just keep complaining about salt shakers with three holes, and Mr Bauer. I cycle down streets, trying to take side routes whose names I don't know – but I know every street, or at least one store. I know which classmate of mine lives on this street or that road, it's all familiar; the city projects its map onto the part of my brain which weaves places into my DNA. If I were blindfolded, I'd still arrive at my destination because my body knows the city, and even if I chose to cycle around aimlessly, I'd arrive at my destination, and I'd end up in front of Shahira's arthouse cinema – all roads lead to Shahira.

The cinema's on the first floor, with a small cafe on the ground floor. I walk up and see Shahira leafing through a magazine be-hind the counter. She reads very slowly, her gaze strained.

'Hello,' I say, as neutrally as possible so as not to startle her.

'Raffiq? What are you doing here?' She gets up too quickly; I startled her after all.

'I don't know.'

'What happened? Is Younes okay? Where is he?' She gets up and comes towards me, bringing her worries with her.

'At school probably.'

Shahira relaxes but her gaze is still strained; she's trying to read me. Whenever I stand in front of her, I notice she's only slightly smaller than me. It always surprises me: both the repetition of my thought and her size. We sit down at a small table in the corner.

She starts speaking Kurdish, says I should tell her everything. But I can only tell her everything in German. I don't speak Kurdish with Shahira, because my vocabulary and grammar are at the level of a five-year-old. Even the English I learned at school is better than my Kurdish. My English teacher wouldn't believe me if I told her my shitty English is better than my mother tongue. I don't tell her; I don't tell anyone. I speak German with Shahira because her German's broken, not as broken as my mother's German, but she slips up. She's aware of her mistakes but can't correct them because she doesn't know how to. I have the means, but I withhold them, so I can finally be at eye level with her; only when she bends down towards me can I look her in the eye. Usually, she speaks Kurdish, and when she does it's suddenly obvious why all the men fall for her: the world hides in Shahira's mouth. But today she listens to me; it's uncomfortable how focused she is. She usually only graces Younes with this much attention when he's sad.

'It's probably a good opportunity for your father,' she says in the end. 'And probably for you too – you're your father's son. I couldn't live there, and I wouldn't want Younes to either.'

'Why not?' I ask.

'As a young girl I really wanted to ride a bike but I wasn't allowed to.' I don't want to imagine Shahira as a child; that's impossible, I want to tell her, you can't have been a child.

But she keeps talking. 'My older brother taught me in our courtyard. When I took my bike outside, the boys whistled at me. I was only ten, I didn't understand why those little boys couldn't stand seeing me on the bike.'

'Do you know now?'

'Can't you guess? Raffiq, you need to stay here,' she says. For a moment I think she wants to swap me for her son, send him to Frankfurt so I can live in his room, so I can be with her. But she has no idea about Younes' plans.

'You have every option here, there you'll be restricted,' she says.

'Maybe that's true in your case.'

'Do you think you could go out with your girlfriend and fool around like you do here?'

'That's not the reason I don't want to go there.'

'What's the reason then?'

'I can't speak Kurdish.'

'You'll learn. I managed to learn German.' I don't want to speak Kurdish the way she speaks German, but I don't tell her that.

'It's not perfect,' she says, 'but I only need one language to think.'

'It's not just the language. What am I supposed to do there? I don't even know what to do here.'

'There, you won't have the luxury of not knowing what to do. You do what's offered to you. You're young, intelligent, you're a man. You can do anything you want here. No one's stopping you.'

'That's the problem. I have so many options I don't know which path's the right one. If you have something concrete, then you can work on it; if you give me an assignment, I can do it.'

'You need to come up with your own assignment. That's freedom, Raffiq.'

Maybe I just don't know how to deal with freedom.

It's true you don't need a heater in the winter when Shahira takes care of you. Younes was never cold, because Shahira rolled him up in several beige woollen blankets, and she rolled me in blankets too, laughed, said we looked like lambs, and we bleated and told her how freezing we were, just for fun, and Shahira threw more blankets on us, making our faces disappear. We stopped talking, and Shahira wiped away the beads of sweat forming on our foreheads, and she called us the cocooned, the veiled, the shivering, and she grew quieter and quieter, and I heard only the touch of her lips, and a ghost lived in Shahira's body, speaking in a foreign tongue: a poem or a story, a thought or a surah, and we slept in dense darkness.

In the evening father seems resolved. He only says what's absolutely necessary during dinner; at least he's not picking a fight. My mother knows nothing of his plans, or maybe she does. Maybe the thing with the mobile was her idea, maybe I'm just imagining things, maybe I think I'm more important than I am.

'I was on the phone with Anwar today,' says father. Anwar's his younger brother in Zaxo. 'He wants to open his own office and wants me to join him.' He's only now telling my mother – she's as clueless as I was this afternoon, and hearing his idea exposes her emotions.

'How can you join him when you've got a job here? Are you getting time off?'

'No. He wants me to work with him over there. I'm going to work as an architect again in Kurdistan, I'll be practising my profession.'

Mother eats more slowly, she drinks, and I can't read her facial expression. She doesn't look happy. Suddenly I'm autistic, unable to read between the lines, unable to interpret my mother's wide eyes, her constant nods, her wild wandering pupils.

'I'm not going,' I say, turning their attention towards myself. I don't want to keep looking at my mother's face.

'I'll come!' Newroz exclaims, thinking we're talking about a trip to an amusement park.

'We're all going, honey,' father says. 'Your brother's just a bit confused.'

'Newroz, you're not allowed to ride a bike there,' I say, trying to make her understand the consequences of moving; she's just passed her cycling exam and is really proud.

'Why not?' she asks. She looks at my father in confusion.

'Because you're a girl!' I say.

My father shakes his head. 'He's playing with you. You can ride a bike as much as you want there.'

'Until another car bomb explodes. Then it's over.'

'That's enough!' shouts my father. Now my mother yells at me too; a minute ago she was undecided.

Newroz gets up, runs off and cries: 'I'm staying here!'

My mother accuses me silently, no words, everything's unclear for now, she's suddenly floating, my father's turned her into a hot air balloon. She gets up to console Newroz.

'It's decided, Raffiq.'

'You can't decide for us. We haven't talked about it.'

'What do you want to talk about? I've been asking you for years what you want to do here. At your age, I was already making major life decisions.'

'And I have to make my own decisions.'

'You can't stay here on your own.'

'I'm moving in with Younes. We're going to uni in Frankfurt. We've already found a flat.'

'You won't stay here on your own. Especially not with that boy – he'll have a bad influence on you.' I know he likes Younes, but suddenly he's a bad influence because his divorced mother sleeps around.

'A bad influence on me?'

'On your behaviour. Two boys on their own in Frankfurt with no parents – that's a sure guarantee for a good-for-nothing life.'

'His father lives there.'

'Not another word. You're staying with your family.'

'You can't force me. I won't work for you; I don't want to be a shitty architect.'

He yells back: 'We've lived here for too long. You're already ruined!'

We stop eating, stare at the rice and sauce in front of us, the sauce already congealed on the edges of our plates. Father's calmed down again and is trying to convince me, but I get up and leave. Zaxo is 3215 kilometres from here.

***

I meet Jenny at Amca's, whose entire business is dedicated to selling one dish. Almans call it 'Turkish pizza' – everyone else just says lahmacun. It's pointless to talk to Jenny now about keeping Amal here. I need to find someone who has the same influence on my father as Jenny has on Amal. Jenny's already sitting there with a steaming lahmacun; I take a seat next to her with mine.

'How can I help you?' she asks.

I'm not going to say a single thing about Amal. 'What makes you think I need your help?'

'Because blokes don't just meet up with me like this.'

'Sure, we can just sit here. Eat. Chat.'

'So this is a date?' She smiles and her smile would be hard to notice if you didn't know Jenny.

'Yeah, well, like not a real one,' I say.

'How can I help you, Rareffiq?'

'Can you imagine emigrating?'

She sighs. 'Amal's definitely going to Chicago.'

'I'm not talking about Amal. I asked if you could imagine living in a different country?'

'If it's sunny there. I'm moving to Spain one day to open a cafe that'll sell the most amazing food.' She sounds as if she's the first person to ever have this idea – Jenny, the pioneer.

'Imagine your parents emigrate and you have to go with them.'

Now she's looking at me with eyes wide open, her mouth becoming two angles pointing downwards. She swallows heavily. 'Rareffiq, do you have to go back?'

'Back? Jenny, I was born here.'

'Yeah, but you know what I mean.'

'I'm not a damn fish to be thrown back into the water.'

'Rareffiq, do you have to go back?'

'Back, back! What the hell are you talking about? You sound like my father! You sound just as retarded, Jenny.'

'Hey, keep it down!' Amca shouts from the counter. 'You're bothering the other patrons.'

The *other patrons* is a Black guy hypnotised by his phone.

'Hey you!' I shout at the guy. He looks up. 'Yeah, you!' He doesn't want any trouble, I can tell by his expression; he's willing to punch me if necessary, but it won't be necessary.

'Are you going back to Africa one day?'

'What?'

'Are you going back to Africa one day?'

'I don't get you, man.'

'You're a bit deaf, eh? I asked you if you're going back to Africa one day?'

'No, man. What're you on about?'

'I'm about to kick you out, kid!' Amca shouts.

'Leave it, Rareffiq, I get it.' Jenny puts her hand on mine; it's warm and soft. I'd like to put my head on her shoulder. I bet Jenny's good at consoling.

I haven't ruined her appetite; she keeps eating. I roll up my lahmacun and take a bite.

'What are you doing after graduation, Jenny?'

She speaks with her mouth full. My mother would make her shut up with one glance; first chew, then speak.

'I'm going to be an au pair too.'

'Was it your idea?'

'Don't you want to know where?'

'Where?'

'In Chicago.'

'You're going together.' Now I get why Amal's so confident – it's because of Jenny.

'I'm a bit scared, Rareffiq.' She takes a large bite and looks outside, as if she's scared of the world out there.

'I looked at Chicago's crime rate. Some people call the city Chiraq.'

'What does that mean?'

She's a bit embarrassed to explain it to me. 'Chicago and Iraq. Because of the Iraq war.' She speeds up her eating, stuffs her mouth full so she can't talk any more.

'And you guys want to go there?'

She shrugs, gulping down her food in order to answer.

'I wanted to go to Texas,' she says and notices how ridiculous it sounds. Jenny probably dreamed of swinging a lasso on horseback when she was a little girl.

'A cowgirl.'

She grins.

'I like it,' I say.

She grins.

Strangely, Jenny's wish, which sounds like a childhood dream, as pure and naive as it seems, fills me with satisfaction.

'You should go there, Jenny – it's sunny there too.'

***

Sanye's consistent. She hasn't changed since I've known her. Unlike Jenny, she's stayed the same in a healthy way. In the same way a tree constantly grows while staying put, and the more the tree grows the more beautiful it becomes, and the more it grows the stronger it becomes – and branches sprout out of other branches, and its foliage rustles in the wind, and you know the tree's there, and the foliage provides shade in the heat, and the foliage exhales oxygen, and the tree's a tree. Sanye will stay with her mother; she won't do a year abroad like most of the girls in our class. Instead she'll stay here and grow here. She's proof that Amal's wrong. The world's the same everywhere, Sanye proves it: there are trees everywhere, water, and clouds moving – that's all you need to know about the world. When Amal talks about places, she speaks about meeting the people there. But people are the only thing that make places unreliable, the only thing that doesn't define a place. If Younes moves to Frankfurt, he'll remain Younes because Shahira still exists; because what happened, happened. His past lives on inside him, his past made Younes what he is today. In Frankfurt he can hide all that from others, but at night in bed, the past will lie heavily on his chest, and it'll contract his lungs a little more every night until Younes leaves Frankfurt as well.

And if father thinks he can build anything of permanence in Kurdistan as an architect, he's wrong. A war could break out in Kurdistan next week and crush all its buildings – what remains are the trees, the water, and the clouds. What remains is Sanye.

Sanye is planning a pre-graduation party at the lake, at a beach house you can rent there. Sanye has a list of people who want to join the party, it costs twenty euros each. No one asks her what the money is for; everyone trusts Sanye. I look at her while she adds names, crosses off others. Sanye has had the most beautiful handwriting since primary school – no one can compete.

64

Amal storms towards me. 'Why do you always ruin things that are none of your business?' She lights a cigarette, flails her red nails about in front of my face. She's wearing black leggings, even though it's cold; her skin partially shimmers through.

'Aren't you cold?'

'Why did you do it, Raffiq?'

I don't know what she's talking about. In a few months she'll be in Chiraq, and I might be in the real Iraq. I need to find out how many kilometres lie between us, how many time zones, and if we'll ever see each other again. Her shirt barely covers her arse, and Walid checks her out as he walks by. I could flip out now, or I could take a handful of her butt, whisper in her ear, and let her believe everything's cool between us. After all, all the girls wear these leggings; it's like a new school uniform, paired with red lips, heaps of mascara making it look like flies got caught in their lashes, hair ironed flat like curtains.

'You can't bear it when you're not needed,' she says. 'When people make plans without you. You want everyone to walk around with a list like Sanye, asking you if they can add your name.'

'I have no idea what you're talking about,' I say and grab her hand; I want to hold her close, she must be cold.

'You talked Jenny out of going to Chicago.'

Well, that was easy.

'She wants to go to Texas now. Fucking Texas!' she screams and pushes herself out of my embrace. 'Do you know what there is in Texas?'

'No, what?' I ask.

'No idea. No one gives a shit.'

'Jenny gives a shit.'

'Jenny doesn't know what she wants.'

'And you do know what she wants?' I ask. 'Did you even talk to her, listen to her?'

65

'Since when do you care about what other people want?'

'Since always.'

Amal avoids me for the rest of the day. She picks Jenny for her team during PE class; she'd rather lose than have me on her team, and Amal's a sore loser. And because Amal isn't on our team, Walid has the courage to comment on the girls' bodies. He says Jenny's a waste of a body, that's how he puts it, 'a waste of a body' – if it were up to him, he'd reassemble her body to get a better result, put some thigh fat into her butt, the softness of her belly into her breasts, glue her arm hairs onto her eyelashes.

'You're a fucking psycho,' I tell him.

'You are, Walid,' Younes agrees. Walid disgusts us and we agree he should definitely not be at the lake party.

'He's got the potential to be a serial killer, that retard,' I say to Younes. But Younes isn't in the mood to talk about Walid and asks me if I've thought about his proposal.

'How do we pay for our own flat?' I ask.

'We work. We get student loans.' He's looked into it. 'There's so many options.' He sounds like his mother when he talks about options.

'I need to know, Raffiq, are you in or out?'

'My father wants me to study in Iraq.'

'Is that what you want?'

'No, mate,' I say and avoid making eye contact. 'Does your mother know about your plans now?'

'It's none of her business.'

'You just want to run off?'

'Raffiq, it's not our parents' choice. For the first time ever, it's our decision. Why don't you get it?'

'Frankfurt isn't your choice – your father lives there.'

'Raffiq, we'll meet new people, see new places, we'll go to Italy over the summer, we'll work, we'll meet new people.'

'You already said that.'

66

'Yes or no, Raffiq?'

At this moment, I realise Younes needs me, just like Amal needs Jenny in Chicago; he needs me. He doesn't know anyone in Frankfurt, not even his own father, and he'll need to learn to navigate strangers' stares.

'I'll come with you, alright?'

Mother and Jamal's wife are stuffing vine leaves in the kitchen. They fold them into small, fat rolls. Their voices are low – mother's telling her about father's plans, and Jamal's wife listens to her, her face soft like whipped cream.

'Make yourself a sandwich until the food's ready,' mother says to me.

'I'm not hungry.' Jamal's wife looks at me with pity, thinks I'll be in Kurdistan in a few months, forgives me for not greeting her. Mother continues whispering as I go to my room. Newroz is sitting at my desk, drawing something. She knows she's not allowed in my room on her own, but she ignores me – as if all rules have stopped applying since father's announcement. Guests are no longer greeted, privacy's no longer respected, and I detonate car bombs during dinner.

'Get out.'

She leaves my room without protesting, still doing what she's told. That's how we were raised; we do what we're told. We do what father and mother tell us to do. And father can overrule mother; the opposite rarely occurs. I should be able to get mother and Newroz on my side. We have to stand up to father. He can go to Kurdistan on his own. I look at Newroz's drawing. She's drawn on my chart, the words *Life Goals* and *Expectations* float above her drawing: a family outside a house. Newroz has summarised all her expectations and goals in one simple drawing. She's good at drawing; she must get it from our father. Maybe she can be an architect and work for him in Kurdistan, even if it means she can't ride a bike any more. A bit of injustice in her childhood might inspire her.

***

Someday the world will stand still, if only because Shahira wants it to. She'll be able to tell me why mother and Newroz shouldn't want to live in Kurdistan, even if they don't know they do yet. With Shahira's help, I've learned to read people. I know Younes by heart. Amal tries to make it difficult for me, but I can read her too. I underestimated my father; I ignored the first rule Shahira taught me: pay attention to how someone comes home, what they bring in from outside.

Nothing happens when I come home feeling sad. I know, I've tested it out. My mother doesn't notice; she gets me to take out the rubbish or go and buy olives, as if it doesn't matter that I'm sad. Shahira reads people; my mother just reads Jamal's wife. I don't remember if she ever hugged me when I was sad. But I don't want her to touch me; her hands are always wet because she's permanently washing dishes. She'll make friends with another woman in Kurdistan, maybe a woman who's married to a man called Jamal. But in Kurdistan there's no Younes, no Shahira – they can only exist here, they're only possible here.

I ring the doorbell a few times before Younes opens up. When he sees me, he tells me to come in, and runs back into the living room and onto the balcony. I follow him; Shahira's on the balcony too, and both are looking down at the town square, now the scene of a brawl.

'What's going on?'

'Jamal and Ramsy are beating each other up,' says Younes.

Shahira looks down at the scene in horror: two bodies bashing each other, not with precision but with power. We don't hear fists striking flesh, fists ripping open skin – we just feel our guts squirm. Shahira flinches with every blow. She fears the fight might disfigure her lover Ramsy.

They sweat, they fight, they spit, they become one. A couple of men have the guts to pull Jamal out of the fight, but Ramsy starts insulting him, calls him a dirty dog, and Jamal, the dirty dog, uses his last strength to pounce on Ramsy again, the lower part of whose face is red with nose blood. Ramsy collapses to the floor, way too skinny to stand up to Jamal's weight, and although Jamal isn't much broader, he still seems stronger than Ramsy, has more energy, moves quicker. But now five or six people intervene and try to break the two apart. Kids swarm around the fight. Some laugh, not realising what's going on. Jamal's son stands confused with his friends, and I really don't care about the kid, but suddenly I hope nothing happens to that dumb fuck Jamal. I wonder if Jamal's wife is watching her husband fight Ramsy the cashier in the town square. I look at Shahira again, who seems frozen as she watches the scene unfold.

'I wonder what they're fighting about.'

Shahira looks at me, frowning. 'Is that important?' she asks.

'It's the most important thing.'

'It's probably because of some dumb card game,' says Younes, his attention still directed towards Ramsy and Jamal. We can hear police sirens in the distance; they'll take their time to get here. Eventually the two bodies are separated; both have trouble staying on their feet and walk in disoriented circles – it's too late to leg it. The police arrive and run towards the men, arresting them; Ramsy falls to the ground and doesn't get up again. Two policemen give him first aid. Jamal staggers towards the police car in the grip of an officer, yelling insults in Ramsy's direction, only he doesn't actually yell in Ramsy's direction – but everyone knows who he means, and they don't hold it against him. In the evening, the blood will be dry and black, a few boys standing around and telling each other who saw what. They'll re-enact the fight between Jamal and Ramsy, hurt each other for fun. One of them will scream too loudly, the police will be called again, they'll ask the boys for their IDs and then send them home.

We go inside, sit on the sofa in silence and smoke. Shahira's shaking, trying to hide it through quick inhales, but she's already smoked two cigarettes since we sat down.

'What's up?' Younes asks. He's noticed her behaviour too and can't take it any longer. 'What's going on with you?' he asks again, because it's obvious she didn't hear him the first time.

'Nothing, my love, the fight just shook me. Seeing two people attack each other like that, seeing how they can hurt each other. Doesn't it scare you?'

Younes is satisfied with her answer, but he doesn't know about Shahira's affair with Ramsy. I just don't get how someone like Ramsy manages to sleep with Shahira. His scrawny body shows a lack of respect, his bony fingers defile her. I would've hit harder in Jamal's place.

Shahira's thighs are made to be touched, round and soft without jiggling; you want to touch her, reach between her legs, make her giggle and tremble, but then she might ambush you and swallow you whole. So many curves that ask to be considered. I can't imagine any man taking her, desiring her in such a way that she'd never pine for another man again. I think Shahira's looking for a man with fifty eyes and three dicks to desire and satisfy her. She'll keep whoring around until that man appears. We'll keep calling it whoring around until we understand that Shahira belongs to another species; she's a new kind of being, maybe a mutant – thirsty, only satisfied by a man with three dicks and ten litres of sperm, but not by a cashier called Ramsy.

Shahira goes to bed early; the fight left her scattered and it's impossible to have a conversation with her.

'Can you imagine what it feels like to beat someone to a pulp like that?' Younes asks. The TV emanates a blue light onto

70

Younes' skin, lights up his muscles, which he only puts to use in the boxing ring. Younes can't afford to flip out.

I nod, yes, I can imagine. 'Shall we go outside?' I ask.

'Not today.'

I love the neighbourhood in spring; when the sun shines longer; the days are endless; when April's rain makes the streets shimmer black; when the street lamps' orange light is reflected in asphalt puddles; the brake lights, the off-licence lights, the betting shop's neon signs are reflected on the wet street – then the neighbourhood transforms into a galaxy. The cafes set up white plastic tables on the pavement; there's a faint smell of kebab meat when you cross the street; the heat from the charcoal grill wafts out when people leave the shop; the laundrette pours steam into the air from a barred vent, coating those passing with the smell of detergent. Some friends laugh loudly at a shisha bar, and the Turkish baker sells his last baklava. Two homeless guys sit on a bench holding a beer and a hot lahmacun, glad to have survived the winter.

I go to the guys in the shisha bar and ask if they know the reason for the fight.

'There's just rumours,' Majit says.

'It's not just rumours, man,' says his brother Maher. 'My father said Ramsy flirted with Shahira. Ramsy's useless as soon as Shahira's in our shop.' Maher uses tongs to free a cube of coal from ashes. 'Jamal somehow found out and flipped out; he's apparently hooking up with her too, wanted to save her honour – as if you could save a qahba's honour.'

'Qahba's honour. Good song title,' Majit says and jots it down in his phone.

'Jamal?' But he's married, I almost say, as if that matters. But he's a loser, a gambler, an annoying neighbour who makes stupid comments, he's Jamal – I get Shahira less with every passing day. Before the cigarette smell and the shisha smoke latch onto my clothes, I say goodbye to the guys and go home.

71

Jamal's wife is sitting hunched over on our sofa, crying into a tissue while mother strokes her back. Her son Bilal sits on the other end of the sofa like a stranger, studying his fingernails with a strange look of guilt. His fingernails have lines of dirt running beneath them and he's using his thumbnail to scrape the dirt out; I want to tell him it's not his fault Jamal's his father. My father's a bit further away from the women, but his elbows are propped up on his knees and he's talking to Jamal's wife. She shouldn't believe the rumours, Jamal's a good man, he says. And she contradicts father's defence by revealing how late Jamal comes home at weekends, sometimes not at all; he empties the bank account and doesn't give her any money, she has to beg him, she says.

'It's no way to live.' She repeats the sentence until we forget what it's supposed to mean.

'I always suspected he had something going on with that woman.'

And my father can't argue with that.

Jamal's wife forgets her gestures and facial expressions; she just cries and won't stop, no matter how often my mother strokes her back; she cries until her entire face is wet, and her face still looks wet even after she dries it with her hands, even after father passes her fresh tissues. Bilal purses his lips, his eyelids no longer sluggish; he's awake and pressing himself into the couch. I put my hand on his shoulder and tell him to come with me; he shakes his head. I fool him with the age-old trick that I've got something for him in my room. We go to my room, and I look around to see what I could give a ten-year-old to play with. I turn on my computer and put on 'Fifa'. He sits completely lost in front of the screen, and then he looks at me.

'I don't want to play,' he says. 'It's for kids.'

'You are a kid.'

He seems to think about it but doesn't touch the mouse.

'Do you want to watch a film, maybe? Or do you watch any TV shows?'

He shakes his head.

'Everyone watches something. What do you watch on TV?'

He shrugs his shoulders.

'Okay, then I'll show you what I used to watch.' I type *Chip 'n' Dale* into YouTube and tell him about the rescue rangers: they're two chipmunks, one's serious, the other's a chump. I always wanted to be Chip – the cool one, he wore a felt hat and a brown jacket. 'But Dale was funnier, and I think I turned out to be Dale.'

Bilal doesn't laugh, just looks at the floor, so I keep talking: 'Their pet's a fly called Zipper. The rescue rangers solve crimes; they're detectives. I wanted to be a detective too. They save people, sometimes even the whole world.'

'Is my father going to jail?'

I don't know but I just answer: 'No, the police will just ask him a few questions, and then he'll come home.'

'His nose was bleeding.'

The tension leaves his body, and he cries, folds his arms together on the desk and hides his face. He reminds me of Younes as a kid when he cried at the school's Christmas breakfast. His crying was just as quiet, loading the same weight onto his skinny back. The posture, the weeping, the delayed breathing – a timeless choreography: that first cry caused by the pain adults trigger in each other. Trigger pain; such a strange term to distance yourself from another person's wounds. I go to the window and look out because the crying won't stop while someone's watching. Younes only stopped crying once the teacher took him outside.

My father's an obnoxious bastard; he talks about Kurdistan when Jamal's wife and son have gone home. He says people get corrupted here, there's no decency here; even grown men can't control themselves, he says and looks at me.

Mother says, though absently – probably reason has come over her – people are no different in Kurdistan. 'There is strife and pain everywhere.'

'You want Raffiq to stay here with no one taking care of him, no one raising him, no one showing him right from wrong?'

'I know right from wrong.'

'You're a child.'

'Why are you talking like we're leaving Raffiq behind?' asks mother. 'We haven't decided yet if we want to take this step.'

'I thought we had,' says father.

Mother shakes her head. 'I told you I'd think about it.'

Father empties his chai glass in one gulp and says, 'I'm going with or without you.' He gets up and leaves the room.

My mother doesn't say anything.

'I'm almost eighteen.'

'You'll always be our child.'

'Your son, not your child.'

'Raffiq, don't forget, we're not German; we won't just leave our child because of some number.'

'It's not just a number. It's time. It's eighteen years.'

'I just hear eight and teen. You're just a teenager.'

'He'll give in, just don't give up now.'

She looks at me with reproach; she's good at that. She looks at your face without saying a word for five seconds, goes completely rigid, and then she closes her eyes and turns her head to one side and stops looking at anyone, every word swallowed by her silence – you can hear yourself, but she makes every word sound banal; she's a black hole and you have to be careful not to stay in her presence for too long. Just as I'm about to leave, she says I'm out to make her an abandoned woman, a Shahira. She says: ne-sakini – an indignant, an impatient, a non-waiting woman.

Shahira's one who doesn't wait, a woman who's not containable. And mother speaks of divorce and says: ber-dan – to let someone free, to stop holding someone down. The words lose their meaning when I translate them.

I watch an episode of *Chip 'n' Dale* on YouTube, the episode Bilal missed. Who knows how many things he'll miss out on because Jamal's his father, how many opportunities will pass him by, how many things he won't know.

The other day a father picked up his son from school – the boy was maybe in year six, and his father came by bike; they walked ahead of me, and I heard them talking to each other like two grown-ups. I followed them for a while because their conversation was interesting: the father explained the difference between a requiem and a symphony to his son, and they talked about Mozart, about the boy not liking his music teacher, and his father told him he shouldn't hate Mozart's requiem just because he doesn't like his teacher. I thought that was a really sensible thing for a father to tell his son.

YouTube recommends other videos beneath the one I just watched. There's a documentary about American bombs – *Little Boy and other Nightmares Made in USA*.

A grey-haired bomb expert explains how the most expensive bomb in America works – it's hardly ever used, but if it is used, it strikes with hellish precision. That's what he says: hellish precision. '*Each of the 250-kilo explosive devices is set to detonate directly over the target to unleash its most lethal effect, which comes more from overpressure than from tearing up the victim. The vacuum created by the explosion sucks the air out of the lungs, while the shock wave crushes bones and ruptures or melts the internal organs of anyone within 50 metres.*'

The grey-haired bomb expert nods at the end of his description, looks past the camera glumly, probably at the reporter, and nods as if his neck vertebrae were loose. I scroll down, read the comments, and most of them are from Almans who want to be funny.

Where was Muhammed when the bomb fell? one of them asks and gives the answer: *Everywhere.* 122 likes.

Alman two comments: *Knock knock, who's there? Not Muhammed.* Only 36 likes.

Alman three comments: *What's the difference between a Pakistani school and the Taliban headquarters? No idea, I'm just flying the drone.* 72 likes.

Ibo comments: *You bastards! Children are dying, it's not funny.* Only five likes. I give him a like.

'So, what'll it be? Torn apart or melted to death? Two very different methods of destruction, right?' I ask Walid the next day.

'A bomb tears you apart. Melting sounds harmless, like chocolate.'

'True, a melting stomach probably doesn't hurt; it melts away really slowly,' I say. But Walid doesn't pick up on the sarcasm.

'No, no, melting's different than melting away. Melting away's faster. When something melts away, it's no longer there, and when something melts it's still there but in another form. Chemistry, year eight,' he says. I hate it when people do that: state a fact and then the school year, as if the whole world remembers what nonsense you learned in year eight.

'It doesn't make a difference if a stomach melts away or melts.'

'It does make a difference.'

'It makes a difference if a stomach tears apart or melts. Those are two types of pain.'

'You'll be long dead by then; you won't even know what's happened to you,' he says. 'Stop, mate, you're depressing me.' I don't tell him about the jokes. Younes comes up to us.

I was late to school this morning to avoid walking with him. I didn't turn around once during class. I went to the bathroom during break, and just nodded at him quickly. Now he greets us both and Walid says he needs to see the secretary.

'What's up with you, are you avoiding me?' Younes asks.

Most people don't understand you, even if you dissect your own body in front of them. Younes just needs a few glances or non-glances, an unspoken word, a missing handshake in the morning. 'Are you having doubts about Frankfurt?'

'I don't know if I want to go to Frankfurt with you,' I say.

'Mate, what the hell? I already told my uncle we're coming. You can't just change your mind every day.'

'I can't base my decision on your uncle.'

'I don't get you,' Younes says, looking as if I've betrayed him.

'My father won't let up.' And your mother doesn't make it any easier.

My parents are in the living room, sitting there just like the night before, and mother's been crying. The wrinkles on my father's face are deeper, and they'll stay; in the future they'll remind me of how my parents sat in the living room, as if they'd been there for hours, sharing thoughts every now and then, falling silent again, crying, hands cramped up until the pain in their fingers numbed their skin.

My father looks at me and tells me to take a seat, his voice thick.

He asks what he can offer me to make me want to come with him to Kurdistan.

'Nothing. I want us to stay here,' I say, and I look over at my mother, who looks back at me. My father nods, but not like the bomb expert in the film; his nods gradually decrease and turn contemplative. It's quiet; I can hear my own breath.

'What do you want?' he asks.

'I just told you, I want to stay here.'

'I didn't ask you what you want here, I asked you what you want regardless of all the places in the world.'

77

I think about a bunch of things, but no answer will satisfy him. I think of Amal's chart with Newroz's drawing, I think about the arthouse cinema – I could help Shahira there; I think of how I could help people follow their heart's desire – like Jenny going to Texas or Majit becoming a rapper. I'm good at that. I could become a manager or a coach. And because I can't explain any of this to my father, I lie: 'I want to meet new people, I want to go to Italy over the summer, I want to work here.' I just repeat Younes' ideas.

'That doesn't sound like you, Raffiq,' father says.

'Babu, if I study here, I'll have a German degree and then I can work anywhere in the world, including Kurdistan.'

'But you won't, you'll stay here. If you do your degree in Kurdistan, you'll want to work there.'

'Oh please, you can't compare a German degree with a Kurdish one.'

He laughs listlessly; he sounds distressed. He's got this reaction from German authorities often enough, when telling them he's an architect. Father's eyes are focused on a distant point, on his past, on the week he spent in his bedroom after he finally gave up the idea of becoming an architect in Germany. That week's what destroyed my father, and now I understand why I don't want to go to Kurdistan; the thought repeats in my head like an idea that's existed long before any of us did, but it only now occurs to me.

'In Kurdistan, I'll become what you are here.'

That's all I say, I don't talk about failing; my father knows what this sentence contains, and the sentence lies in our living room like a corpse; we all stare at it, and my mother's the first one to make a sound. I look at her, and she smiles – it's the smallest smile in the world, a trace of a smile, but it's enough.

***

We call it a beach party, but actually we're just at the lake. The city poured a bit of sand on its banks; it feels like fake grass. The lake's small, as small as our world, but we still call it a beach party. Everyone wants to be close to the lake, to sit up at the front, to stare into the water, expectant, as if wanting to regress and live underwater, where words go unheard. The final exams are over and we're partying to pass the time before we get our results; the boys are in charge of the barbecue, and the girls take care of the food. Sanye's running the show; she bought sardines, which we line up neatly on the barbecue like soldiers. Sanye drizzles lemon juice on them; she squeezes half a lemon into her hand, and the seeds stay between her fingers while the juice dribbles onto our sardines. She puts finely chopped parsley on the fish – I also smell dill and mint – and squirts on wasabi out of a tube. We can't get enough of the fish, and someone says, this must be what mermaids' fingers taste like, and Sanye laughs and gives us bread and says it'll satisfy our hunger, but we stay hungry. Someone puts music on and we put on our sunglasses, Jenny dances with Amal, the sun caresses our shoulders, it's obscenely hot for May – and May should go on forever – and then we start telling lies: we should go to a Jay-Z concert – and someone says he's in Berlin right now, and we could smoke shisha in Kreuzberg, and we should spend the summer in Havana – I get the shivers from feeling so happy. Jenny brought a shisha – we smoke it, and no one can tell us what to do, we're here and we're loud, eating our sardines with lemon and parsley and wasabi, which burns in our noses, stings between our eyes, and Sanye's dancing now too. Younes seems careless, keeps dipping his toes into the sand, mounds stay on his feet and toes, small pyramids, the sand must be tickling him, and I touch the sand with my fingers; it's warm and soft. You could sleep on this sand.

At some point Sanye and Younes dance together in a close embrace, and you want to stop and look at them; it's like being in a museum, you really want to understand what it is you're looking at. All the others dance around them like ghosts, their bodies now transparent because Younes is moving with Sanye.

I concentrate on the girls' legs. They inaugurate the summer with their short dresses, the hollows of their knees all sweaty from dancing – they've no idea how beautiful the hollows of their knees are, the transition from calf to thigh; most guys probably just look at girls' arses, yeah the arse is important too, but the backs of the knees are really intimate, they almost look breakable when they bend, and most girls are ticklish there. Every area of skin which makes a girl laugh is more interesting than her arse, which feels good to touch, but I think most girls don't feel anything on their arse cheeks, because they don't react at all.

Shahira exposes her rounded white calves when she lies face down asleep on the couch in a short dress. Her thick white calves aren't toned, they look soft like breasts, and once I touched the back of her knee with the tip of my finger, and it woke her up; she looked at me, confused, and I apologised. She mumbled not to touch her when she's sleeping.

I only start drinking once the sun has set – alcohol keeps you warm, says an Alman, and I want to tell him I know that. Someone makes a bonfire, and now everyone's looking for wood to add to the fire, and someone says, 'Stop messing around, it can't get too big,' but the girls laugh and throw branches onto it. I sneak up on Amal and hug her from behind; she's all warm from dancing and from the fire. She's giggling, she's in a good mood – soon you'll be in Chicago, I tell her, and she hugs me. Amal and I fit together so well you need a key to unlock us from our embrace. No one at the lake has the key, and Amal lets me touch her everywhere; and when it gets dark, we look for a spot away from the drunk, laughing group, and we lie down in the grass, and my hands are invisible, and she lets me touch her.

'It's almost sad we're breaking up, we're so good together,' she says.

'We don't know if we'll still be good together in five years,' I say.

She looks surprised but pleased. 'My God, Raffiq, you sound all grown-up.' I stick my nose in her hair, and then I smell her neck, kiss her, and my hands stroke every curve – I want them to be able to remember when Amal isn't here – and this moment lasts for ages, and she's stopped giggling, she's had a lot to drink, I've had a lot to drink, and what Amal's best at is licking my neck with her tongue, her breath on the wet part of my neck gives me goosebumps on my arms and legs. Amal's the wind carrying you to another city. We ignore that the others have long since finished the barbecue and left, we ignore the fire merely glowing red now and the sun dipping the moon in yellow, the grass cold and unruly. Ifrits rise from the lake and return to the water when they see us; it doesn't bother us that people die and others are born. I love Amal at this moment – not as Amal, but as a human being, as a divine gesture.

We fall asleep.

We're woken by homeless people collecting deposit bottles from the party. Their laughter's a warning to get dressed quickly: I shield Amal, so these hungry mouths don't devour her body.

'Look at his small dick! Girl, if you're in need of a good fuck then...' He doesn't finish the sentence; the punchline is his floppy, swinging dick with foreskin. His friends laugh.

I walk Amal home; I can do that because Amal only has a younger brother. Her father spends most of the year in Kurdistan; Amal doesn't speak about him, he doesn't exist, 'It's just me and my mother,' she says, and she doesn't allow any questions – she's strict about that. She denies me one last kiss at the door; I'm unsure if it's because of my breath or hers. I want to tell her I love her, but I don't know if it's true, I just know I'd like to speak the words.

She walks up the steps, gently; her body must hurt too from sleeping on the ground, from all the dancing, from the alcohol.

I want to call her name, so she'll turn around – but I don't, and she doesn't.

I'd like to ignore my phone, but I need to know how angry my parents are, and I can tell by the amount of times they've tried calling. They've called seven times, the last time at 2 am.

My parents and Newroz are eating breakfast when I come home. The sun shines through the window, gilding the air and feigning peace.

They stop eating for a moment and look over at me.

'Where were you?' asks my mother.

'At our pre-grad party.'

'What's that?' she asks.

'Obviously a party where they get drunk out of their minds,' says my father, and diverts his attention back to eating.

I join them, and Newroz is grossed out, says I stink; I breathe on her, she shrieks, and I kiss her on the cheek.

'Leave her be,' says father; he doesn't tolerate silliness at breakfast.

***

Younes and I always go to the gym on Saturdays, but he hasn't been in touch; he's probably recovering from last night, even though he doesn't drink. He says he wants to stay in control. If my father heard that, he'd trust Younes to live with me.

I add a pair of pants and socks to my sports bag already containing shower gel, boxing gloves and sneakers. My bandages stink; they need washing. I see Jamal smoking outside and we nod at each other, no words. A blue bruise embellishes his left eye, his nose is a bit bigger than usual. I unlock my bike.

'Still not got a driving licence?' He laughs. No idea what Shahira sees in him, honestly. I turn around and look at him closely; his cheeks are freshly shaven, his hair's full – you've got to give him credit for that – but his shoulders are no wider than mine, his chest's flat, his hands are almost boyish, the abrasions on his fingers are crusty. He's probably a good-looking guy.

'What are you staring at?'

'Why did you beat up Ramsy?'

'None of your goddamn business.' He drops his cigarette butt, steps on it gingerly and goes inside. He'll be asked this question a lot now – he could've prepared an answer. But Jamal's a liar; he'll tell everyone a different story, and the incident will be forgotten in a week's time because something else will happen for people to gossip about. Jamal won't let it go though, and I'll always think of Shahira when I see him. Shahira swallowed him whole, and he's another one condemned to stay in her belly – none of us will ever forget her, we'll worship her and compare every woman to her, and we'll realise: Shahira isn't human. She belongs to no one; we should be grateful for her presence.

The punching bag buckles when Younes hits it with his right hand, and when he wants to reach a certain state, he pounds the punching bag over and over. A group of boys stand around him. You can't walk by without wanting to stop for a moment and watch Younes keeping the punching bag in motion. Younes' training defines what our training goals will be. A song's playing in the background, fragments of conversations or groans emerge from corners, but what really dominates the room is the squeaking of his shoes on the floor. He once told me he thinks best when he's boxing, when every muscle's twitching, when his big body's in motion, and he just doesn't know what it is that gets his body moving – like an animal, he says, there's an animal in my body; and this animal likes it when the wind touches his sweaty, wet body, making him feel every inch of skin. Younes wants to reach a state of flow, say goodbye to every muscle, leave his body, enter a trance. But he needs an equal opponent to reach that state, he says, and he doesn't have that opponent, he says. Until then, he'll try to reach that state on his own.

I walk over to him, stand behind the punching bag and hold it. He nods me a thank you; I need to get a grip on the leather or else it'll slip away. I lean on it with half my body weight and feel the cushioned punches. The chain clanks.

'When did you leave yesterday?' I ask him. I bring him back to the present moment. He thinks.

'Around ten.'

'That early?'

'Sanye had to go. I walked her home.' He slows down, then stops. He takes off his gloves, asks if I want to have a go.

'I want to warm up first.'

We jump on the treadmill. I'm better at running than Younes, but it doesn't bother him. He doesn't try to beat me. He probably doesn't compare himself to me; he's in a different league. I concentrate so hard on running that I think I'm about to fall. Sometimes I imagine the most impossible of situations, a scene playing out where I die at the end or hurt myself so badly I want to die.

We walk home together after our workout, and we'll always walk home together, even when I'm gone or Younes disappears, even if we're in different places – when one of us walks home the other one will be there too like a phantom. Our muscles are pumped up, we float above the streets, and if we stamped our feet, we might leave cracks in the asphalt.

He asks if I've seen Jamal.

'Yeah, he doesn't look bad,' I say.

'I think Ramsy is worse off.'

'Hopefully. They shouldn't have caused all that stress for nothing.'

'They entertained you, Raffiq.'

I almost tell him about Jamal's wife and son sitting in our living room crying because Jamal's having an affair with Shahira, which everyone knows about now. I almost tell him about Jamal's son not watching cartoons because he was too afraid for his father. But I let Younes believe the fight entertained me.

'I'm thirsty, let's get a drink,' he says and points to the MaMa brothers' mini-mart, where Ramsy works as a cashier. Younes' craving for sensation is new. Maybe it's because he thinks he's not involved in any way.

'You want to see Ramsy?' I say.

He shakes his head. 'No, I just want to get a coke.'

I don't believe him, but I go with him because cold coke's the only thing that can quench my thirst. This fragile figure is standing at the cash desk, his veins like green and blue wires, his face oily; his eyes are black and huge, his lower lip's swollen and split open, his nose is bandaged. Ramsy stares absently at the floor, leaning his left hip on the cash register. He doesn't notice us until we stand in front of him with two cold cokes. Two rings of water remain on the black conveyor belt as he takes our cokes, and then he stares at the bottles as if he's never seen coke bottles before; he puts one bottle down next to the cash register. 'One euro twenty please,' he says and looks at me.

'I'm getting the second bottle as well,' I say and hand him five euros.

'I'm not serving him,' says Ramsy. We know he means Younes.

'Why not?' I ask. Younes looks at Ramsy in confusion.

'Ask the others,' he says. His lip's so thick and tight it doesn't move when he talks. Yet he's not afraid of Younes; he'd rather risk getting beaten up again than serve him.

'I won't serve you or your mother. Get lost!' There's spit dribbling from the corners of his mouth because Ramsy can't speak and swallow at the same time. Younes sees the determination in Ramsy's eyes. We leave the shop; I offer him the coke and he

85

declines, it's not his to drink, it wasn't sold to him, and Younes picks up the pace. I open the bottle, take a sip, then I point the bottleneck at the ground. The coke foams and fizzes from the bottle's opening – it'll mark the path we walk.

Everyone remembers when Younes first fought back. It was in year seven, the other kid was in year nine; Younes pulled his arm back to take a swing, and at that moment, the wind decided to rush to Younes' aid, and Younes' fist hit the boy's chin; he fell on his arse and just looked surprised, his palms bloody from trying to soften his fall. His mates laughed, didn't help him; it was a kid in year seven after all, for fuck's sake, they said, and the year-nine boy got up and charged at Younes, but Younes stayed put and punched the kid in the face again to prove to himself and to all of us that the first punch wasn't a coincidence. Every boy in the neighbourhood remembers the first time Younes fought back, and he never lost another fight, no matter who challenged him.

Majit cycles towards us. The bike's clearly too small for him; it must belong to his younger sister. He asks if we're coming to the shisha bar tonight. Younes keeps walking, doesn't give a shit about Majit and the shisha bar. I stay put, and Majit just asks: 'What's his deal?'

'Ramsy didn't want to serve him.' My bottle's empty; we both look at the brown bubbles fizzing away in the space of seconds.

'They wouldn't extend his temporary residence permit. He's being deported.' Majit sits on the bike as if on a stool, his knees almost up to the handlebars.

My parents always talk about whose permit didn't get approved and who had to leave as a result, they always talk about it in a tone as if those affected had a disease, cancer – and alhamdulillah, we don't have it – their tone always suggests we could also be affected, and I ask Majit: 'What now?' Even though I know what'll happen now.

'Now he's making himself unpopular. He was cheeky to my father yesterday as well, but my father understands him, didn't say anything.' He clicks his tongue and shakes his head. 'As if having to go back's the end of the world.'

'You have no clue, mate,' I say, and I leave him standing; maybe I can catch up with Younes.

Jamal's son is sitting on one of the big decorative rocks in front of Younes' building. Three bags of groceries are leant against the rock; he looks bored. I wonder if people see my father when they look at me. Bilal just nods when I greet him – no hello, no wave, just a nod like a seventy-year-old. And then he looks away as if I'm not there. I ask him what he's doing here, why he's not taking the shopping home. The bags are packed full, they must be pretty heavy; he can't carry them on his own.

'Come on, I'll help you,' I say and grab two bags.

'No, I have to wait here,' he says; he's suddenly awake and looks at me.

'Who says so?'

'I'm supposed to just wait here.'

'How come?'

He looks at his feet, afraid I can read his thoughts.

'Your mother's going to be pretty mad if the things in the bag go off.'

But he doesn't move. 'Are you waiting for your mother?' No reaction. 'Or for your father? Mate, I can't help you if you won't talk.'

'I have to wait.'

'Okay, then I'll wait with you.'

Some kids are patient, they're brought up to wait. I'm not one of them, I tell him, but he doesn't care.

I look up; the house swings downwards when you look up for too long. I tell him that as well, and he looks up, looks up for quite a long time, it must hurt the back of his neck. Strange boy, really.

I look up again, and only then do I realise who he's waiting for.

No other Kurds live in these flats, no friends of Jamal or his wife – only Shahira and Younes. I race up the stairs; that's faster than the lift.

I ring the doorbell, leave my finger on the bell, hit the door, call Younes. Shahira opens the door, her face a teary mess; she pulls me inside and tells me to hold him back. Younes and Jamal are in the living room, the sofas and the table an island between them. Jamal's pleading as he buttons up his shirt with shaking fingers. He calls him his son, which makes Younes charge towards Jamal, who runs around the table away from Younes.

'Younes! Stop it, mate, it's not worth it.'

I don't know if Younes is aware of me; he's focused entirely on Jamal.

I don't have the courage to get between the two. Shahira cries, tells me to do something.

'Younes, please, mate. Let's go outside.'

'Shut the fuck up, Raffiq.' And I shut up.

This is what it looks like when Younes' body loses control.

'Younes, please come to your senses,' says his mother.

'Shut the fuck up.'

Shahira opens the front door so Jamal can escape. Younes' only weakness is his slowness, but he sees through his mother's plan, runs to the front door, locks it, takes the key, and throws it on the table in front of Jamal.

'Go and get it if I'm your son,' he says to Jamal.

'Younes, please, I want to marry your mother, we're not doing anything wrong.'

'I'll break all your bones, if not today then tomorrow,' he says, breathing heavily. Suddenly Jamal's the reason for all the injustices that have happened to Younes; we all understand Younes' anger, we're all responsible for it, but no one wants to get close to it.

'I'm going to get you, you wanker,' Younes threatens again.

'Enough,' screams Shahira again and again. But that's not how it works.

I want to go home, not see how this will end, but I'm forced to watch. Jamal says something that provokes Younes to run after him again. The little boy's waiting on the rock to go home with his father – he can only guess at what's happening up here, his neck hurts but he ignores the pain, and his skinny legs are numb as they dangle from the rock, his feet almost touching the ground. I approach the table and take the key to unlock the front door. Shahira sees this and inhales deeply, gets ready for her next move.

'Don't do it, Raffiq!' Younes yells. I unlock the door, opening it as wide as possible so that Jamal can escape like a hounded rat. No matter how invincible Younes is, he can always be betrayed. His mother blocks his path and they both slam into each other, Jamal tears down the stairs – maybe he'll fall and break a leg, but he gets away for today. Younes stands in front of me, takes a swing and hits me in the face.

**

I couldn't stop crying, even if I'd wanted to. It's like laughing; you can't just suddenly stop. My parents asked what happened and I couldn't tell them; whenever I tried, I talked about the coke, how Bilal was waiting on the rock, how Younes smashed into Shahira, how she fell to the floor, how Younes punched me in the face – and his punch still burns today. My nose tingles underneath the splint; I want to scratch it, but my mother holds my hand, I'm not allowed to touch it, she says. I help them wheel their suitcases to the check-in counter. They're not going on holiday, they're preparing their return, they say, repeating it; it's a formula to help them understand what it is they're doing. They won't stay there, not forever, I know that. Take care of the flat, take care of yourself, eat properly, behave, shame will still reach us in Kurdistan, don't think we'll go deaf, take care of your studies, that's top priority, they say, again and again, as if I have to learn it by heart. I stop listening; I've seen Ramsy in the check-in queue. His nose is no longer in a splint like mine. He approaches us, greets my father.

'I'm going home,' he says. We pretend not to know about it, because he feels the need to speak. 'They wanted to give me another chance. My lawyer said I'd probably get a residence permit in a few months, but no, no, I'm done. I told them I'm fed up with them and their Germany. I congratulate you on your country, but I want to go home – that's what I said at the immigration office, to the fat cow on her chair. My father's got a hotel in Duhok,' he tells us. If Ramsy were at least a good liar, Shahira could be forgiven for her affair with him. My father just nods and pats him on the shoulder, not wanting to expose him; he knows the truth, but we let Ramsy tell his story. Ramsy doesn't ask me what happened to my nose – it seems to remind him of his, so he refuses direct contact with me. I remind him of everything he's leaving behind.

I always sit at the back of the bus, then I don't feel pressured to get up when an old woman gets on. That way I don't have to greet Kurdish women and answer their questions, either. The bus driver drives too hectically; I get off one stop early and walk the rest of the way. I walk along the street, and maybe I'm imagining it but the buildings duck down, they seem scared as they sit on the street, making themselves smaller; the street's narrower than it was two hours ago, and I know every corner, I know how many street lamps there are and what stickers are stuck to their poles, I know which car belongs to whom – the neighbour-hood's a memorised poem, and somewhere in these small streets with the ducked-down buildings is Majit, riding a small bike and dreaming of becoming a rapper.

My parents forbid me to ask Shahira about Younes. I stand outside her door, half a watermelon in a bag. My nose begins to tingle again, but I know I'm not allowed to touch the splint; I gently scratch the tip of my nose with my thumbnail. The skin's still numb. Shahira looks through the spyhole, and it doesn't take two seconds for her to open the door, call my name and embrace me in her arms, squeezing and holding me.

'I'm so happy to see you, sweetheart.'

'I would've come sooner,' I say and keep the rest to myself. Shahira can guess why I wasn't able to visit her. She asks me to come in and goes into the kitchen; I follow her. Her hair's tied in a bun – she's wearing a sleeveless dress barely covering the backs of her knees. I see she's beautiful even without make-up, more beautiful in fact because it seems intimate, as if she only allows certain people to see her without a mask; she somehow looks naked and in focus. It's an especially hot June, and I remember how she used to spread her legs on the balcony, and I knew she must've sweated between her thighs, her skin sticking together. I place the watermelon on the kitchen table; she grabs a knife and two plates, cuts the melon into crescent-shaped slices.

She asks how my parents are doing.

'I just took them to the airport.'

I can't place her smile as she cuts the melon into red cubes. Her arm movement exposes her armpits; they're greyish, you can see stubble growing, and a single black hair has escaped the razor blade – her armpit reminds me of a pussy.

She asks about Amal.

'She wants to go to Chicago.'

'And you?'

91

'I don't want to go to Chicago.'

'Do you love her?'

'I want her by my side. If that's love…'

'It's one form of love.' She smiles again. 'The most romantic form of love is unrequited love. The pain you feel, it sits in your body even after ten years, the heartbreak grows into your flesh, did you know that?'

'We broke up on good terms.'

'That's romantic.' She pushes a plate of watermelon cubes towards me and sits across from me.

'You've got a nerve, of all people, telling me about love.'

She grabs a red cube and bites into it. Her hands, flawless, as if powdered, guide the fruit to her mouth, and the way she props her elbows up on the table, one hand erect like a bouquet of flowers, nails painted red, you'd think those hands were draped on the table, resting there just to guide food to her mouth for all eternity. The nails, too long for a mother's hands, could hurt a baby's flesh. I was scared of these nails scratching me when I was a kid, and I'm sure they hurt Younes when he was little, when she put cream on him or changed his clothes, and when it made him cry out, she probably just kissed him on the spot where it hurt, and he was quiet, and those hands and those fingers with long nails said: I don't care about you.

'Has Younes been in touch?'

She shakes her head.

'You don't seem worried.'

'I know he's with his father.'

'In Frankfurt.'

'Could be.'

'It doesn't hurt that you've lost him?'

'I haven't lost him. He'll lose his father once he meets him. That hurts me.'

'What do you mean?'

She looks at me, slows down her chewing, thinks about what she can tell me. Her gaze is dismissive, it lingers on my splint.

'I had no other choice,' I say. 'His little son was waiting for him. I had to unlock the door.' Younes doesn't know it, but I didn't betray him. 'You told me I had to do something.'

She doesn't say anything, she just thinks: but you shouldn't have done it. You should've endured the situation, like Younes endured it all these years. Before the crying starts again, I get up.

'I know, Raffiq,' she says, walking me to the door, stroking my hair with both her hands, stroking my face; her nails don't hurt me, and she says: 'It's not your fault, okay?'

I nod.

'What's Younes' father called?'

'Salman. Why? You're not going to Frankfurt, are you?'

'Salman what?'

'Zaxoy.'

'What else?'

I put his name and 'restaurant frankfurt' into Google. I get restaurant recommendations in Frankfurt, but the name Salman Zaxoy is always crossed out. I google 'salman zaxoy kurdish restaurant frankfurt' and get only döner places and kebab shops. One guy has called his restaurant 'Gundi' – there's no way that's a Kurd from Iraq. Some döner places even have cool names: Dönerstan, Dönerium, Dönerday, Main Döner.

I should call and ask if they know Salman Zaxoy; maybe people working at döner shops know each other, maybe there's something like a döner network.

I dial the number, and the phone rings for a long time before someone answers. The guy's annoyed and asks: 'Hello?' No introduction, no mention of the restaurant; it could be a shoe shop for all I know.

'Hello, can I speak to Salman please?'

'Salman? There's no Salman here.'

'Salman Zaxoy, he's Kurdish, from Iraq.'

'He doesn't work here, mate. Is that it?'

'Please. Do you happen to know him, do you know where he works? He has a döner place in Frankfurt as well. Or maybe a restaurant.'

The döner guy laughs. 'You think everyone who sells kebabs knows each other?'

'No, I know there's no döner network, I just thought maybe you know your competition.'

'Our döner's the best.'

'I don't want a döner.'

'Then why call a kebab shop?'

'I'm looking for a friend.'

'Then keep looking,' he says. 'Frankfurt's got more than a hundred kebab shops.' He hangs up. Rude bastard. I call another shop, and another, and no one knows Salman Zaxoy. I wonder what I'd call my kebab shop. Dönerverse, Abra-kebab-ra, Return of the Döner, Silence of the Lambs.

'Restaurant Anatolia Kebab.'

'Hello, can I speak to Salman Zaxoy?'

'Speaking. Who's this?' I was so busy making up names, I forgot what I wanted to say.

'Raffiq. I'm Younes' friend.'

No reaction, as if he doesn't know who Younes is, or as if Younes has told him about my betrayal.

'I want to know how Younes is doing and have a quick word with him.'

He's quiet, apparently thinking what to answer. What's there to think about? I want to ask him.

'Can I please speak to Younes?'

Now he answers quickly: 'He can't come to the phone right now.'

'When's a better time to call?'

'If you're his good friend, why don't you call his mobile?' His father isn't totally dumb, but neither am I. Younes won't reply to my messages.

'My mobile broke, I lost all my numbers.'

'And who told you my name?'

Is he a detective now or a kebab seller? – what's up with all the questions, why's he so suspicious, who does he think I am? He's annoying.

'Younes told me your name. Can you please tell him I called? He has to call me back, it's important, it's about his exams.' I hang up; I don't want to answer any more questions. I look at the restaurant's address; it's pretty close to the main station.

***

I waited for a long time, for a text message or a call. I hoped he wasn't doing well and that he'd call me; his good friend, or maybe former good friend. Frankfurt's a big place, and as the quiet type, it won't be so easy for Younes to find people to talk to. But I know Younes can handle staying quiet for a long time; he can handle being alone for a long time. Out of all of us, Younes is the best prepared to wait an eternity for redemption.

I bought a high-speed train ticket for the first time in my life. I'm travelling on my own for the first time in my life – on my own to a place that's more than a hundred kilometres away. A mother with two small kids is sitting across from me. She reads them a story. The girl keeps looking over at me as if I'm bothering her by looking at the book's cover, as if I'll become part of her memory because I'm listening in, because I know what the story, set on a farm, is about.

My father didn't need a book to tell me stories; the words were part of his thoughts, and he told me a story about a businessman who owned an exotic bird. The bird could talk, and when the businessman planned to visit the country the bird was from, he asked his bird: 'Do you want me to bring anything back for you?' The bird described in great detail where his family and friends lived, described how to get there, and he told the man to ask about the well-being of his kind. As the man really loved his bird, he wanted to do him this favour. So he went to the place where his bird came from and set out on the path the bird had described in such detail, and the man was astonished at how accurate his bird's description was. He arrived at a clearing to find countless birds similar to his own, singing and playing together. The man called the birds to gather around, and he told them of his bird, and the birds listened to him, and when the man asked if they wanted to pass on a message to his bird at home, the clearing grew very quiet. Suddenly a bird dropped from a branch, slammed to the ground, its body stiff and lifeless. Before the man could rush to the bird, another dropped dead, then a third, and so it continued until the branches were empty of birds. The ground was studded with colourful bird corpses. Shaken, the man returned from his journey, and the bird asked him if he'd been to see his friends. Full of grief, the man shared what he'd witnessed. As the bird heard this, his little body stiffened and dropped dead in the cage. The man regretted having told him the news. He carried his dead pet to the garden to bury him. When he was about to place the bird in the hole he'd dug, the bird suddenly flew onto a tree, thanked the businessman for delivering his message and flew away.

'What happened then? Did the bird fly to his friends? Will the businessman visit him?'

'Yes,' my father said so I'd sleep. But I'd sometimes imagine that colourful little bird flying for a long time to reach his friends, and sometimes he'd arrive to find they actually were dead, they hadn't just pretended, it wasn't just a message to the bird in the cage – the news of the caged bird killed them.

I longed for my father to keep telling the story. I wanted to know how the bird reached his friends, I wanted him to reassure me they'd faked their deaths; they could only remain alive through his storytelling.

But he just said: 'That's where the story ends.'

I'm going after Younes, I need to see Younes.

Younes is sitting on the kerb in front of his father's restaurant. A basketball wedged between his feet, he's staring at the other side of the street and smoking. Printed on his white T-shirt is 'Anatolia Kebab'. A young boy, maybe as old as Jamal's son, runs out of the restaurant and stands in front of Younes, apparently wanting his basketball. Younes gives him the ball, points at his cigarette. The boy tries to dribble but lacks the necessary strength, so the ball stays on the ground after one bounce and rolls away. I walk in their direction. Younes frowns when he sees me, stays seated, unsurprised, as if he expected me to come here.

'What are you doing here?'

'I thought you were ignoring my messages to get me to come here.'

The little boy stands next to Younes with the ball under his arm. The way he looks at me already annoys me. 'Younes, who's that?'

'Raffiq, a friend.' He nods slightly in the direction of the boy. 'This is Ayaz, my brother.' Then he corrects himself. 'Half-brother.' The boy puts his arm on Younes' shoulder and tells me Younes can carry him. There's no resemblance between the two, not in their looks, gestures or how they speak, but the boy seems to trust Younes, clings onto him, and Younes lets the boy touch him – only a half-brother.

'Ayaz, go inside and grab us two cokes.' The boy goes, still looking at me, his mouth open, his bottom lip sluggish and wet with drool. I sit next to Younes and ask him if he likes Frankfurt.

'Haven't seen much of it.'

A short beefy man comes out of the restaurant, stands next to Younes with two cokes in hand and asks, in Kurdish, whether we want to come inside. He could be his father; the little kid looks like him, but Younes bears no resemblance to him at all, no matter how long I stare in search of the tiniest detail. There's not a single feature in Younes' face inherited from his father – neither the nose nor the mouth; everything's from his mother, she passed her face on to him to proclaim Younes belongs only to her, a piece of flesh taken from her body. I'd sometimes search his face for an unrecognisable feature to attribute to his father, but I never found any. As if God had thought his mother so beautiful, he decided to make a copy of her.

Younes takes the cokes from him, his gaze still on the street, and he says no, it's too hot inside. Not even their hands, which might connect them, are alike. There's no point of contact.

'Are you Raffiq?' asks the man.

I get up, hold out my hand, try to smile, and Younes' father seems to go on shrinking. This is the man Younes waited so long for, this is the man Shahira was married to for ten years, the man she cheated on, the man who lured her to Iraq, this is the man who dropped Younes off with his mother and never returned. He doesn't smile, he doesn't have wrinkles, neither around his eyes nor on his forehead – his face is expressionless. This man's such a stranger it makes me go cold. When he goes back into the kebab shop, I sit next to Younes again, both of us silent. I can't talk to him; we smoke a cigarette, then another, we empty the pack and get up with tarred lungs, the kerb warm now from our bodies; we walk along the street and Younes doesn't speak.

'I'm sorry. I shouldn't have opened the door. I'm really sorry.'

We walk towards the station; actually I'm following Younes, he's dictating the speed and direction.

'I have to get out of here.' And I think he needs to get out of here too, he should forget that man with no facial expression.

'She told me to get lost,' he says.

'Who did?'

'His wife. She doesn't want me here.'

'Who gives a fuck about her, mate, as long as you're with your father?'

He shakes his head.

What's happened, Younes, what did you experience these last weeks without me? I want to ask him, but his silence and evasiveness prevent me. Younes is ashamed, and his shame increases because I'm here to see his shame. He's ashamed he can't live with his father either, even less so than with his mother. Younes goes into a Chinese restaurant, says he'll be sick if he has to smell onions or veal again.

We sit down in the darkened restaurant, order noodles with chicken.

Younes' stepmother came to him on his first evening in Frankfurt, with a cold stare and stiff lips. She asked him if he had any idea what his father had to endure because of his mother. She ambushed Younes with her directness; he didn't say anything, because she expected him not to – he was just supposed to listen, and Younes listened. He was actually curious to hear the other side of the story at last, imagining his father, that beefy guy, shaking in bed late at night, suppressing tears and pain. His bride lying next to him; she can only guess what his ex-wife must've done to him. She doesn't have the courage to ask him about it for a long time.

So Younes waited, mouth slightly open, anxious to hear his father's story; spellbound to finally feel connected to his father – at least in suffering. They'd both suffered for a long time because of a woman, but now they were free.

The stepmother looked at Younes' face, a face utterly unfamiliar to her, and at that moment she knew Younes' features belonged to the woman her husband had tried to forget. Now she'd reappeared, had smeared her face on this boy's face – here's my face, go and open some wounds.

'You need to leave. Go back to your mother and leave us alone. You can't ever come back.' She didn't wait for an answer. If I'd been with Younes then, I would've put my hands around her neck until she couldn't speak another word.

Younes understood the hatred was directed towards his mother and not him, and he wanted to explain that to his stepmother, wanted to console her, tell her she was mistaken, he had nothing to do with the pain his father had endured – but she shook her head, cried and told him to be quiet and go back to his mother.

A few days later, his uncle suggested he stay with him.

'We don't have enough space,' his father said; it wasn't an explanation, nor an excuse. He didn't want to hear any complaints, and he said it while slicing tomatoes, not looking at Younes. It wasn't worth having eye contact over, just one sentence: we don't have enough space. Younes understood. He'd put his father in a difficult situation, and he wanted to make things easier for him. It's not a problem at all, he told his father, really, I can live with Uncle Azad.

He was allowed to help out in the restaurant during the day – that way his stepmother didn't have to endure the sight of him.

Once, he sat down for lunch with his father and his uncle. They talked, and Younes spoke about his A-levels and his future plans. His father's face remained unchanged, and he asked Younes about his mother, what she was doing, and if she was still a whore. Younes chewed his bread until it lost all its flavour, turned to mush in his mouth. His uncle tried to change the subject, but his father insisted on an answer. Younes looked at his father, nodded, and his father turned away from Younes in disgust.

'I hate him,' says Younes. It's the first time I've heard him say that. 'I wish he'd never existed.' Younes is relieved after saying it. He takes his father off his back, and we keep walking. His father doesn't exist, not now, not then, not in Younes' face. Shahira created Younes. She just had to make everyone believe she needed a man, but he grew up in her belly because she wanted a son so badly, and she called him Younes.

***

Younes and I stand in front of the town hall, a seven-storey building with large black-tinted windows; we walk in and look at a board displaying all its departments: registry office, immigration office, citizen's service. The resident registration office is on the third floor; we take the lift. Younes has the rent contract rolled up in his left hand. I tell him off, say the contract looks unprofessional. He unrolls the document; we look at it, make sure our names are on it: under the word 'tenants' we see our names. Both our first names are spelt incorrectly, there's an f missing in my name, and Younes is missing a u, but whatever, says Younes, our last names are correct, and the person in charge won't care. What matters is we've got a place, he says. I find it unprofessional, but Younes just tells me to chill. We enter a room with a lot of people waiting with rent contracts, and we also sit down and wait. Someone waiting tells us to take a number; he points at a screen with neon yellow numbers. We get number 94, thank this considerate man for letting us know, and then we wait a long time – but we don't mind.

I tell Younes the story of the businessman and his bird, and I tell him how the ending always upset me because you don't know if the birds actually did die. Younes nods, says, 'True, it's not a very nice story.'

'Most importantly: will the bird make it all the way back to his friends? It's a long journey.'

'Yeah, maybe something happens to him on the way.'

'An aeroplane engine gets him.'

'He gets eaten by a vulture.'

'There is an ending,' says Younes, 'but what your father told you isn't the ending.'

The number 94 flashes on the screen, and we get up.